CURSED IN THE HOOD

JAE TENE

ACKNOWLEDGMENTS

This is book six for me and to be honest I am very proud of myself. I want to dedicate this novella to my nephew MJ. This book was extremely hard to write because I had lost my imagination and my will to be creative with my pen. While I struggled, MJ stood by my side constantly giving me ideas and making me watch different shows to get my brain going. Michael, you have always been Auntie's inspiration, and I want you to know that no matter what your dream is it will come true. This is for you, auntie baby!

To my readers, I hope you guys enjoy this book, and you check out more of my work. This book is nothing like you have ever read, and it will have you looking around to make sure no one is watching you. Open your minds and let your inner kid take over. Cursed in the Hood is about to blow your mind!

Check out more by Jae Tene on Amazon and follow me for more releases:

Queen City Hustlas: More Than A Hood Romance 1&2

The Plug and His First Lady
When a Block Boy Loves You Back
Once Upon a Hood Love: A Greensboro Fairytale

Oh, and it's always #MLPP Ladies LET'S GET THIS BAAAAAAGGGGG!

1 / FIONA JUDE

STRETCHING my body and easing my eyes open, I was met by the sun. I loved to wake up to it being bright and early and today was also a big day. I was finally opening up my shelter for the homeless, a dream I shared with my late fiancé, Marco. I thought Marco DiMenez was the love of my life. After he passed, every single skeleton came to haunt me day to night. While we were together, Marco treated me like a queen. Anything I wanted, I got, and I became spoiled. I could admit that. Marco's love was real, and I did know that.

Marco was gunned down during a drive-by with a rival gang that he used to be in. He moved away to get out of the mess, but still had the tattoos and the shit caught up with him. I remember the countless times I begged him to have them removed. I mean we had the money for it, and it was nothing to take the days to get it done, but he refused.

"This is apart of me, Bella. Please do not worry me about those things," Marco would say calling me by the pet name he gave me, meaning beautiful.

My given name is Fiona Jude, and everyone called me by my last name. My father Felix Jude raised me. He was a strong black man that I loved with all of my heart. When I say my father was my world, I meant it. We always met for Sunday and Wednesday dinner, but throughout the week I would always pop in to check on my old man. Marco and my father had a great bond, and I think my father really liked him for me. My mother was white. I didn't know her name, and her face I couldn't even guess. I guess she was a white version of myself because my father would always say I looked just like her, and if I wanted to see her, look in the mirror because that was where I got my beauty from.

My mother and father were dating when she got pregnant. From what my father told me, she was an amazing woman and was excited about giving birth to me. She named me and set up my room, but when he was on the way to pick us up to go home, the hospital called and said my mother had checked herself out and left me behind with a note for him.

My father also told me that he was hurt and didn't know when he would be able to look at me without feeling like he had let me and her down. Growing up, I never heard him bad mouth her or say anything negative about my mother. Around age sixteen, I stopped worrying about that woman. My father was everything I needed, and where he couldn't give advice, he would call his little sister Tasha, and she would give me the run down.

My auntie was the shit, but she always was overprotective and deep in the game. Thanks to her I was too, but I didn't touch any drugs, I was too pretty for that shit! I had seen what drugs do to people, and I didn't want to ever mess with that shit in any way shape or form. I would clean up though. I had been cleaning up her messes since I was eighteen, and my father never knew. That was the one secret I kept from him, well second.

Six weeks before Marco's death, I found out I was pregnant. I had only told Marco, and I prayed he didn't reveal it because I wanted to surprise the families. After his death, I set an appointment for an abortion and never looked back. I was hurt, and it was the biggest mistake ever. Marco was so excited about the baby, and I was too, but

I was also afraid. My father was getting older, and he was gone. I had told Marco firsthand that I wasn't ready, and he reassured me that together we would raise this child. His death brought on more fear because it wouldn't be him and me. I would be a single mother, and that wasn't fair to me. I was selfish, and to this day I regret it, I wonder what the baby would have been and how he or she would have looked. It haunts me every day, but I have forgiven myself and prayed that Marco did too.

Jumping in the shower, I hurried and washed my ass and got dressed. I wasn't trying to be fancy or anything, and it was chilly outside, so I decided to wear some slacks and flats with a long sleeve blouse. I hurried to get my purse and briefcase and walked out the door forgetting my jacket. I turned to go back inside my house and heard a car pulling up. I turned and saw it was Gravy, Marco's best friend.

"Jude, you about to dip?" he yelled from the window, and I nodded and hurried in to get my jacket.

I walked back out the door, and he was still there. I walked over, and Gravy was looking really good in his all white. He smiled and licked his lips, and I rolled my eyes.

"What boy, it's cold, damn?" I bent down and seen he had his son Josh in the car. "Hey, Auntie's baby!" I squealed and ran to his side to give Josh a quick kiss.

Josh was two, and his mother left him like mine did. That bitch was ruthless though, and when she is caught, I want to fuck her up for Josh and Gravy! She had him, left the hospital in the middle of December, and left that baby on the doorstep hollering. If Gravy's nosey neighbor wasn't watching, Josh could have died, and that would have killed me. Serena was on borrowed time because we would find her ass, one way or another.

"You open today, right?" Gravy turned to the back seat and asked me, and I nodded. He looked just like the nigga from *Notorious*, and they shared the same nickname.

"Facts, let me drop your nephew off, and I'll be by there to support. You look nice, ma." Gravy winked and pulled off, and the wind hit my ass rushing me to my Camaro.

Getting the heat popping off, I started my fifteen-minute drive to Burlington, North Carolina. I only stayed in McLeansville, so it wasn't a fifteen-minute drive, but I was a cautious driver when I needed to be. The businesses and farms were a nice sight some mornings, and I wanted to enjoy it every morning the Lord blessed me with. I wanted to get to the shelter early and start housing people. I knew someone would be there waiting, and I wanted to be there for them.

The shelter that I had built was five stars for the residents, and the money was all coming from an account that Marco had saved millions for. We didn't live extremely lavish, but Marco had us set. I sold the house soon after he passed, but only moved a few miles away. A fresh start was needed. The shelter had workers, three kitchens, and even five dining areas. It was four floors, and the rooms were built like a studio apartment on the first floor. The second floor had the two-bedroom units, and the third and fourth floors help the larger families in three bedroom units. For the much larger families, they had two bathrooms as well, and if they didn't want to go to the dining area, they could order in food from any floor. We had specials that we made, and I was in the middle of an apartment complex deal so that I could help even more families.

I was pulling into my parking spot when my phone rang. I saw my father and me and answered putting my car into park.

"Hey, daddy!" I squealed.

"Hey baby girl, I just wanted to say how proud I was of you. This is such an amazing thing you're doing, and I can't wait to see you when I get there. I know you already in there throwing orders." My father chuckled, and I slowly closed my door. He knew me too well.

"You were close, daddy. You know me, huh? I just got here, and I needed this phone call. I can't wait to see you either, I'm nervous, and I hope they love the building," I said, taking deep breaths.

"Did the furniture and comforter sets come in for the assistance store?" he asked, and I had forgotten to even make sure.

"Daddy, I have to call you back," I said, and he stopped me.

"No, I handled it. They called here just to make sure they set everything up so that the families can pick what they want. It was a huge order so you might be assembling for a while. I gotta go, baby girl. My date is here," he said, and I looked at my phone to make sure I heard him right and that I was still talking to my father.

"You're bringing someone? This is new to me, daddy," I said not trying to ruin this for him, but he never looked at another woman or spoke about one in my entire life.

"Fiona I don't have to tell you everything, and I wanted to make sure she was what I needed first. I've been moving so much better, and I want to start coming over for dinner at your place. When you meet Miranda, you will love her. I know you will."

I could hear the care in his voice, and I didn't want to let him down. I smiled to make sure he knew I was with him one hundred percent.

"That will be perfect, daddy. Let me get this store and these families set up. Auntie Tasha and Stephanie are here already, so I'll see you two when you get here. I love you, daddy!"

"I love you more, baby. See you in a bit," he said and hung up.

I hurried to the front door and saw a Latino woman and her two babies standing in the cold. She was beautiful, and when they saw me approaching, the kids wrapped to the mother tighter, and I smiled warmly.

"Hello, you guys come with me, and we can get you situated." I smiled unlocking the door and letting us all in. "Are you hungry?" I asked the babies, and they looked at their mother, and she nodded for them.

"Yes, ma'am," the oldest spoke up, and she was too cute. I looked over and saw Stephanie wearing a warm smile, and the youngest looked back at her mother again.

"It's okay, mija. Go ahead, and I'll get everything ready for you guys." She smiled, and the little girl ran off to Stephanie with her big sister.

"Thank you so much. It has been a cold fall this year already, and it's only October." She smiled weakly, and I smiled with her.

"Yes, ma'am, I hope you guys stay long enough to enjoy the Halloween activities I have planned. Our staff will also assist with any of your needs. Do you want to go see the room?" I asked, and she nodded.

I took her to see the room, and she was amazed. The girl's rooms were pink and teal, and they both had twin-sized beds. They had dressers, and the rooms came with socks and a card to come to the store and get clothes. Stephanie, my best friend, was in charge of the store. Steph was a true booster and had so many cute outfits for the kids and everything for their parents and even the liners who came in. She carried clothes, bathroom needs, shoes, and accessories. Stephanie was the truth when it came to this project, and I was so glad that she could help out. She also helped Tasha on jobs and was usually the person to call me to come clean up.

After getting the family situated, I went to make sure everything was ready for the rest of the residents coming.

"Girl, is that Gravy's fine ass right there?" Stephanie asked while we placed the comforters up. I turned and saw him still fly as fuck and licked my lips.

"Yeah that's him, and if you hurry and help with all this stuff, we can both go and speak," I joked, throwing a pillow at her dazed ass.

I understood why she wanted Gravy because he was sexy as fuck. I just would never consider looking at him in that way because he was more like a brother to me, and that would be so wrong of me. I can't say that we both aren't tempted because truth be told I was supposed to hook up with him, but he never made it to our date, and I don't wait on no man. Marco came and told me he wouldn't make it and enjoyed dinner with me. After that, we took things so fast that I couldn't tell you when I fell in love with Marco.

"Who is that bitch looking lost as fuck? She needs help but

doesn't look like our kind of help. Look," Stephanie said with her nose turned up.

I looked up and wished I hadn't. It was Miracle, Marco's baby momma— that skeleton that haunts me since he passed. I rolled my eyes as she made her way over to me and got myself ready. I didn't want to ruin this great day, but I would clean this place with her ass if she wanted me to.

"There you are, Fiona. This is nice. My baby daddy really paid you up good, huh?" she asked, and I ignored her ass.

"You not going to answer her, Jude?" Stephanie giggled, and I looked up at her and smiled.

"Answer who? Unless it's my father behind me, I don't owe her a thing," I joked, and I heard him clear his throat, and with the look that Stephanie wore, I had to turn extra quick. I almost lost it seeing her with my father's hand around her waist.

"Surprise!" She squealed giving him a peck on the cheek. I was dumbfounded because this didn't seem right at all.

"Daddy, do you know who this female is?" I asked, looking at her like the dirty bitch she is.

"I do, and I am grown. I know you have had your issues with her in the past, but it's time to let that hurt go baby girl and live. Marco wouldn't want this!" he said, getting stern and it took all of me not to disrespect my father.

"Yes sir, well you enjoy that while I remove myself for something more important. I wish you two the best, I guess," I said and walked to my office.

I didn't have the energy to hear their response. I needed a blunt and a shot of anything strong to make it through this. I pressed the button to lock my door and turned my camera on in case someone came back to get me. I rolled my blunt and right before I lit the tip there a knock at the door. I could see Gravy's ass looking dead in my camera lens, and I burst out laughing. I got up and quickly opened the door and watched his large frame walk in and take over the room. His fresh cut and low trimmed beard were asking for me to sit on his beard and rub them waves. His arms looked like they could lift me while he ate straight from my fountain of youth baby!

Clearing my throat, he turned and smiled, and his teeth looked so damn white that I knew he was trying to set me up. I had to klink, klink real quick because I wanted him to throw me on my desk and punish this pussy for all these thoughts.

"Was that your pops with Miracle? The nigga still got it, huh?" He laughed, and I didn't see shit funny.

"Get out, Gravy. I don't have time for your jokes. At this point, I think the bitch wants any man in my life." I lit my blunt again and pulled so hard that I knew I would choke. Gravy sat down and watched me smoke, and I couldn't read his expression.

"Damn, I wish I didn't hit that lick back in the day. You would still be mine!" He shook his head walking around me. I watched him walk around and got curious. Maybe it was the weed, or maybe it was just me, but I wanted to know.

"What do you mean I would still be yours? I don't know why you didn't call instead of sending Marco's ass. I can't believe he had a baby with that bitch on me, man," I said still heated.

"That was the least, man. He made his mistakes, but you loved him at one point, Jude. Don't bad mouth that man now that he's six feet under. I know it's is a lot to take in, and if anything, take all the time you need. You can't revolve your life around what he wanted because he gone, and it won't change a thing."

He walked over to me and got in my space. I could smell his cologne, and it smelled so good.

"You gotta move on, ma." I looked up at Gravy, and he was stone serious.

"I know, I will. On another note, you still coming to the Halloween party, right?" I asked hoping that he was because Gravy had the DJ I wanted and everything, and I could really use his assistance.

"Hell yeah, you still having that voodoo bitch coming?" he asked, taking the blunt from my mouth and taking a pull.

"The voodoo witch you meant, nigga! Yes, she is still coming, and I'm excited because I haven't thrown a party in so long. Stephanie will be there too," I said, and he shook his head.

"Cool, but my eyes are on somebody else." He looked me over and licked his lips.

"Gone head boy before we get ourselves in some trouble. I'm grown, and I can admit that I see you Gravy, but I don't think that would be best," I said bluntly as hell. There was no need to provoke him as much as I liked it.

"Jude, nobody is checking for your nappy headed ass. I just don't see myself with Stephanie. Nice try though," he said and stopped at the door. "If I wanted you Jude, that back would have been broken in, ma. I'll catch you out here," he said and walked out the door.

I ran to my office bathroom and wet a rag wiping myself clean. Damn, Gravy had me wet as fuck. I had to stay away from his ass because I was two seconds from snatching his big ass back inside my office to fuck me silly! Once I was clean, I changed my entire outfit to a nice black dress and went back to the residents.

━━━

By the end of the night, we had twenty-five residents in our system, and they were all happily in two dining rooms enjoying each other's company. Stephanie thought we would have to break up two baby mommas, but they actually came together by the end of the night for the kids, and that made me happy. It was hard watching my father and Miracle together, but it was what it was, and like he said, he was grown. Now I knew why he didn't tell me he was dating because he knew I wouldn't approve.

Everyone was leaving, and Stephanie came over to help me get things back in order while the residents went to their apartments.

"Girl, you good? I know you tired, but how you feeling?" she asked, and I knew she was referring to my father and Miracle.

"Yeah, he got this and to see him up and out makes it easier. I mean if he is happy then so be it. I didn't know Miracle other than that she fucked my man behind my back. I never exchanged words with her ass until now, but I saw everything that was said about me, so I will never address her. If he wants to stay happy with her, then he might want to keep us as far away from each other as possible," I said with a slight shrug.

"I hear you because I will surely drag that hoe. Speaking of hoes, why were you and Gravy gone for so long? If he didn't have to get Josh, he would have moved your ass into an apartment." Stephanie giggled.

"Girl, we both have a whole house to fuck in if we needed that. I just needed to get myself straight. He was just extra company. I couldn't take it there with him, girl. That wouldn't be a good look."

"Fuck anyone's thoughts, Jude. If he makes you happy, then you will be missing out trying to make everyone else happy. That isn't fair to you," Stephanie said, and she was right, but I didn't think it was fair to Marco either. No matter how dirty he did me, I wouldn't do the same to him.

"I hear you, girl. Fuck, I'm tired, I think I'm going to let them finish this shit up, I need to get ready for this party meeting tomorrow. I only have two more weeks until the party date. I still have to take the deposit to the witch tomorrow, and I'm excited!" I squealed.

"Well, pick me up when you go. I wanna meet her too. I have a date tomorrow night, so that's perfect. She can tell me if I should go or play sick on his ass," Stephanie joked.

"Okayyyyy!" We high fives and finished the job we started. We ended up cleaning everything and letting the workers go to bed.

<hr />

When I finally got home, it was almost midnight, and I was dog-tired. I lit another blunt and ran a bath. I laid in my bed as the water ran smoking and thinking. Gravy invaded my mind, and I wondered if we would even be a good match. He was so sexy, but he was also smart and caring and always knew what to say and when. That was even before Marco passed. I shook the thought and went to turn the water off. I wouldn't want to give myself any bad karma messing with that man. I soaked in the tub and then got in the bed with nothing on. Nothing was holding me back as my body drifted off to dreamland.

2 / GRAVY

I WAS SITTING in my candy apple red Maserati when I heard a slight knock at my window. I looked up from the book I was reading. Jude sat there thick as fuck. Her face was red letting me know that it was cold and she was ready to get in, but I liked to fuck with her.

"What I say about tapping my car, brah?" I questioned, and she quickly backed up and walked to her Camaro. I was bugging because she was stubborn. My phone was right here, so she could have said on the way out or something. I didn't play about my car.

"Man, come on!" I yelled, and she stopped inches from her car and threw me her middle finger. "When?" I countered, and this time she turned to me with a smile threatening to pop out.

"Gravy, why you playing? You know it's cold, and my face turns red when I get too cold," she replied, getting in finally and looking around.

"Why you looking all in my shit like you my girl?" I laughed and pulled off.

"I don't want to be sitting on no used condom or anything," she joked, but I didn't see shit funny.

"If Joshua's going to ride in my car I wouldn't do that, ma. Plus, you know how I am about my cars."

I was a car fanatic. I had an old school box Chevy that I was working on bringing back to life. It was going well. I just had to wait on a few parts from China, and then I would be good to go. My passion was to build cars and sale a few and keep a few. Marco was helping me when he finally moved down and his past caught up to him. To this day, Jude thinks he walked away from the game, but he never did. Marco was so deep in that getting out was not an option. It was also said that the money he saved up was stolen money from a plug, but they never found where the money went. I had to give it to my boy he was smart as fuck to hide that shit the way he did because they still haven't found that shit.

"Hurry up before I'm late. We still have to get Stephanie," Jude said all in her phone.

"I didn't agree to get her, so she is going to have to wait until we get done with this witch doctor," I said, taking the exit off to the witch office.

I didn't know why Jude was so fascinated with the idea of a witch, but I wanted to make sure she was safe. I had heard some shit about this witch, and she was accurate as fuck when it came to reading palms and shit.

When we finally get to the location, it was dull and ugly, and it fit what she was doing in this bitch. I was a little uneasy about going in, and Jude could see it all over my face. I didn't fuck with that voodoo shit. I served the Lord, nothing else.

"Gravy, don't bitch up on me now nigga." Jude put her hand in her hips and looked at me sideways, and I gave her ass that same look.

"Man, come the fuck on man! She does anything to me, and that's your ass, Fiona, I mean that shit!" I walked past her and held the door open for her. Jude thought this shit was funny, but I didn't.

Looking inside her shop, I didn't see anything out of the way. As a matter of fact, I didn't see shit. The building had one table the in the middle and a beam around it. I saw Jude sit at the table and I stood behind her when a beautiful African American woman came from the back. She didn't have on anything crazy either. She looked like a regular hood chick. When she sat across from Jude, she held out her hand, and Jude took it. The woman looked deep into Jude's face and snatched her hand back quickly putting us both on edge.

"What's wrong? I am just here to pay you your deposit for the party," Jude said, taking her money out of her bag.

"You are powerful, sweetie. You have more power than myself. You don't need me," she said, and I shook my head. I wasn't playing with her ass.

"Man, don't pay her shit, I ain't seen nothing that would tell me she a witch or even know how to play the role!" I boomed, and as I turned a swift wind knocked my big ass into a chair that I never saw and slide me beside Jude. I ain't gone lie a nigga was shook, and it was clear a day.

"I know that you have a son Joshua in childcare right now, and he is handsome like his father. He misses you and is giving the care aid Beverly a hard time right now. If you need to go, I understand," she spoke softly and had a smile on her face. Seconds later the daycare was calling, and I could hear Joshua in the back screaming. I looked up at her as I took the call and chills ran through my spine.

"Damn, you are good," I heard Jude say.

"You will be better. When should I be at the party, Fiona?" she asked, and Jude looked at me.

"Wow, I told you my name was Jude, how did you figure out, Fiona?" she asked.

"I heard him shout it outside that wasn't the gift." The witch laughed, and Jude laughed with her.

I stepped out because I had had enough of both their voodoo shit for one day. While I was reassuring Ms. Beverly that I would be there in a few, Jude walked out and got in the car not saying a word. I hopped in behind her and pulled off.

"So, she is most definitely worth every penny. I am so excited!" Jude beamed, and I looked over at her. to see her happy made me calm down a little even though I wasn't as excited. At the same time, I was worried about Josh. He never gave Ms. Beverly a hard time. I was starting to think that bitch did something to my son but shook the thought off.

After getting Joshua, I took him to my mom's house and dropped Jude off at Stephanie's crib. Since the party was one two weeks away, I figured I had enough time to back out and find something else to do. The energy I felt at that store was no joke, and I didn't play about that voodoo shit. Jude had always been interested in it, and what the witch said caught my ear. Jude was powerful and more powerful than her, to be honest, that shit scared a nigga because the witch scooted my big ass in that fucking seat like I was a little nigga. I had to hurry and come up with a plan to get out of going to this party with Jude, fuck that voodoo shit!

3 / FIONA JUDE
A WEEK LATER

"Steph, the party is only a week away, and you expect me to calm down?" I shouted in the costume store we were shopping in.

"Fiona, you better calm that shit down, I was just asking why are we shopping now because it's other things that aren't done. You have been on the go since leaving that damn witch, are you straight?" Stephanie asked me, and I nodded yes.

She was right because since I left, I have been feeling differently. I wake up in the middle of the night every night at 3:15 a.m. and be sweating like a man in my bed. I always have the change my sheets and shower, but I can never get myself back to sleep until it's time for me to get up. I was dog-tired, and I just wanted this party to go well, but I had a feeling I needed to talk to the witch again before this party. If that bitch did something to me, I need to know what.

"Sorry, girl. I have been going through it since then, and I was thinking about going to see her ass anyways. I didn't want to last minute shop for anything because you know how I am when I get like this," I joked, but Stephanie didn't budge.

"Well, you need to fix that shit ma cause it's starting to affect our friendship. My hands are itching to pop your ass the next time something reckless comes out your mouth." She fake smiled, and I rolled my eyes.

"Damn it's like that, huh?" I asked, and she quickly grabbed me and yanked me out the store and to her car. She stood in front of me, and for the first time, I saw real fear in Stephanie's eyes. I was getting chills just from the look alone.

"Yesterday you cleaned up for Tasha and me, but I forgot something behind and came to get it. You remember me shaking you and calling your name but nothing else. Fiona, you were staring at the body parts and saying something. I don't know what the fuck you were saying, but it scared the fuck out of me. There is no question that something is going on with your ass. I'm worried about it too, man," Stephanie said, and tears streamed down her face.

I reached out to calm her, and I could see her slightly back up against her car. That hurt me because she really was afraid of me. I knew something was off because I don't remember any of that just her shaking me, and I thought I had fainted, but I was standing. That was the other day, and she never spoke on it again, so I never brought it back up. This was affecting more than just me, and I didn't want it to get out of hand.

"I'll go see her today. I have dinner plans with daddy later, and I need to be better by then. Can you just take me to my car?" I said, and she went to the driver's side.

⸺

When I got to the witches office, I took a deep breath and walked right in, and she was sitting there as if she was waiting for me. She smiled, and it was not returned.

"Look, I know you have done something to me, and I need you to take it back," I said not even taking a seat.

"Fiona, I just opened your eyes to what you are. We are alike you and me, and as sisters, we must stick together," she said still smiling. I was trying to keep myself calm because I wasn't anything like her ass.

"Listen, I don't know what you are talking about, but I have been having nightmares and waking up every night sweating. I black out and can't remember anything. How does that make me like you?" I asked, and she stood making me back up and reach inside my purse. I don't give a fuck what type of power she had, Marco didn't allow me to leave without my gun. She would feel me today!

"You are waking your inner witch. Soon your powers will erupt, and you will understand. I will see you next week, sister," she said, and I blacked out.

—————

I woke up to someone banging down my door. Reaching to my side table, I grabbed Marco's loyal .22 and hopped out my bed.

"Jude! Jude!" I heard Gravy and hurried to open the door. He rushed in and paced the floor.

I was still distraught because I didn't know how I got home and in my bed. The last thing I remembered was standing face to face with the witch. I walked over to Gravy and put my hand on his chest, and we locked eyes. He calmed down instantly, and his face softened.

"What's going on?" I asked, and he pulled me over to my couch.

"Serena is back and trying to get custody of Josh. This bitch sent the police to raid my shit saying I slang dope. They took him from me until the investigation is over. How the fuck can they do that when I am all he knows, man? I fight day in and day out for my lil nigga, and she can just step in and take him?" He was bugging out and then broke down.

I had never seen a man so broken. He reminded me of my father, which made me remember that I didn't meet them for dinner. I made a mental note to call him first thing in the morning to apologize.

"Gravy, listen to me, I got you! She will not get custody of my nephew as long as I have breath in my body. I know there is something that we can do. As for that bitch, let me handle her ass. I don't need you locked up behind her then Joshua stays in the system." I rubbed his head, and he looked up at me. I wiped his tears, and he just looked at me.

"I don't know why I believe you when you say this shit will be okay. I just want my son man. Serena never gave a damn about him, so why now? This some bullshit, ma," He said, and I nodded.

"But we will get through this don't worry." I smiled and kissed his forehead.

Gravy pulled me further down and kissed me then looked at me. I didn't want this to happen, but my eyes and my body definitely did. He hungrily kissed me and caressed my body. It was as if my body was on fire as he kissed every inch of me. Gravy removed my robe and saw I was only in my boy shorts. Ripping them off, he threw my legs in the air and began to eat my pussy. I arched my back, and he licked all over my clit and then softly sucked on it. I felt him put two fingers inside my pussy, and I moaned out in pleasure.

"Damn, Fiona," he groaned, but I was seconds from an orgasm, and I wasn't hearing shit. I rotated my hips against his face and fingers until I was cumming. I couldn't contain myself, and I needed more of Gravy. I needed to feel him inside me now!

I pushed him back, and the force was crazy. I lunged on top of him and damn near ripped his pants off.

"Slow down, Jude. Damn," Gravy joked, but I was horny as fuck. When I saw his pretty chocolate dick, I damn near slobbered on myself. I guided him inside me, and everything went black.

JUDE WAS SAVAGELY RIDING my dick, and I would be lying if I said I didn't enjoy that shit. Jude was a real freak, and the way she rotated her hips and was throwing her head and arms around made me think she was possessed. I grabbed Jude's hips and tried to slow her down. I was about to nut, and I didn't want to cum early on her, but the way she was riding a nigga I was about to lose it.

I smacked Jude's ass, and she suddenly stopped. I removed her long auburn hair from her face, and she looked scared or confused. I slowly eased Jude off my dick and just looked at her. She was different and calm. She looked up to me, and what she asked me next really had a nigga worried.

"What just happened? I don't remember shit, Gravy," she said, covering herself up with pillows from the couch.

"What the fuck you mean? I was in them guts, and you were riding a nigga crazy. You don't remember any of that shit Jude, and we just stopped?" I asked, and she rubbed her face in frustration. I didn't know what was going on, but I was worried about her. We had just stopped seconds ago, and she didn't recall any of it. I know my dick game wasn't that bad but damn.

"Sorry Gravy, but I need you to leave," Jude calmly spoke.

"Nah, I'm good where I am, ma. I need to make sure you good and with Josh not being at the house that shit just doesn't feel right, " I said, and before she could protest, I picked her small frame up and carried up her upstairs to her room and laid her down. I went to her bathroom and got a warm rag and wiped her pussy.

Jude sat there with her pillow covering her face, but I didn't see anything to be embarrassed about. Just as concerned as she was about taking care of Serena for me, I was going to be there for here through whatever she was going through.

After wiping myself down, I laid down with her, and we just laid there. I didn't know what to say, or if she should say anything. I didn't want to make her feel worse, so I waited for her to either speak up or fall asleep. Either way, I would be right here.

TODAY WAS ACTUALLY A GREAT DAY. There were no blackouts, and I was chilling with Stephanie and Gravy. Stephanie was waiting for her date, Kevon. Kevon was a guy that she met a few weeks ago, and she was just now introducing him to us. Things between Gravy and me were weird, and I didn't know why. I mean we were both grown, and for us to be fucking the way we were, I didn't see anything to be ashamed about.

Recently he would come over, and we would chill, but he wouldn't say too much. Last night he actually had the nerve to ask if I had been around Serena, and I had yet to make it happen. With the shelter and the party, I was literally booked, and it's really had me wondering why he would ask me that. I never asked him though. I wanted him to know that I trusted his timing and I knew he would tell me exactly why.

"Babyyyyyyyy!" Stephanie squealed and jumped onto who I guessed was Kevon.

"Hey, baby," he greeted her back, and they kissed passionately. I felt Gravy caress my leg, but I wasn't messing with his freaky ass. I discreetly removed his hands and stood to greet Kevon.

"Nice to finally meet the man making my friend glow the way she has been." I smiled, and he smiled back.

"It has been a nice little journey. I just look forward to getting to know her a little better." He said keeping his eyes locked on her, and Stephanie just blushed.

"Well, I am Fiona, but everyone calls me Jude, and this is my... uhh," I staggered.

"I'm her uh, Gravy." Gravy stood and shook Kevon's hand.

"Nice to meet you." Kevon laughed.

"So where you from if you don't mind me asking, brah." Gravy went straight in. I looked at him like he was crazy, but he ignored my ass.

"I am actually from Idaho. Small town and small minded people," he said, shrugging it off. I started to get hot and felt a brisk wind come through. Nobody else felt it, and it stopped as quickly as it came. My phone began to buzz, and I saw it was the shelter calling.

Stepping away, I took the call. "Hello?"

"Miss Fiona, I'm so sorry to bother you, but we have someone trying to check in, and they are upset," Maria said. She was the first resident with her two children, and I let her run my reception desk, and she was really good.

"No worries him. I am on my way now," I said, ending the call. I went and filled everyone in, and Gravy decided to take me to the shelter.

Upon arrival, we saw this white woman raising hell and asking for the director. I hurried in, and when she touched me, I felt something but shook it off. When she looked at me, her eyes and face softened. She quickly looked away and tucked her hands inside her pockets.

"Hello, ma'am. I am the director Fiona Jude. How can I help you?" I said smiling as Gravy went to my office.

"I just need a room for a while. I won't be staying long," she said and wouldn't look up at me.

"Okay, no problem at all. We can get you situated here for

however long you need. Let's get your name, and I'll show you to your room," I said, and she finally looked up.

"My name is Cari. I wouldn't like to disclose my last name, and I would really like to get some rest." She said. I nodded and put her single name on a one-bedroom room.

When we got to her room and looked around, and she looked amazed.

"This is really nice for a shelter and for it to be free. Is this what you always wanted?" she asked still looking around and touching the bedding.

"Not always, but it was a plus. I wanted to help people, and this was the best way. People need help, and I want to be available to help them." I smiled.

"Well, I have to go. Just so you know, you are invited to our Halloween party. It will be fun, and it's an adult's party. Try and rest up, and I'll leave your vouchers for our store downstairs on your table."

I left the room, and I could feel my heart racing. It was weird, but I took deep breaths and finally calmed down. Just when I felt myself calm my phone started to ring again.

"Hey, daddy," I sang into the phone.

"Hey, baby girl. I feel like you out there dodging your daddy," he huffed into the phone, and I dropped my head. It was that I was avoiding him, I just didn't have the energy for his situation right now.

"Sorry daddy, but we can have dinner tonight. I plan to have Cherry's Fish and Chips cater for the shelter tonight, and I know how you love their fried lobster tail." I smiled, hoping that would help.

"That will be great, baby girl. We will see you then," he said, and I smiled. I went to find Gravy sleeping on my couch. I shook my head and got to work on the shelter.

Later that evening, I was running like a chicken with its head cut off in my nicest dress. It was fish night, and everyone was so excited, but I was going stir crazy because I couldn't find two children. Maria was calm because she said she had a feeling she would find them, and she had yet to return. On top of everything, the party was in two days, and I had started to see what the witch meant. Unfortunately, she was nowhere to be found.

"Fiona!" I heard and turned to see my father and Miracle coming up to me. She was beaming, and so was he. I decided to let my father do what he needed to do for happiness. If Miracle played him out, then I would step in if needed, but he was grown.

"Hey, you guys." I smiled and hugged my father. Miracle leaned in for a hug, but I was good.

"This is really nice, Fiona. I do want to apologize for the way I came at you at the opening. It was really childish of me, and if you could find it in your heart to forgive me, I would really appreciate that," Miracle said, and I could tell she meant it. Marco was gone, and my father seemed happy, so who was I to stop them when I was just as happy.

"I accept. Our table is right there. You two go ahead. I need to see if I can find Gravy." I smiled and led them to their table.

Gravy had left and said it was an emergency, and that he would call to update me, but I still hadn't heard a thing. I looked around and didn't see him, but I saw Cari coming downstairs in some joggers and a t-shirt. She locked eyes with me, and my heartbeat sped up again. I tried to smile, and she did the same.

"This really is nice Fiona," Cari said, walking over to me.

"Thank you again. How was your room so far?" I asked, looking around and saw my father looking at me like he saw a ghost.

"It was amazing, and the shower was indeed my favorite part so far." She smiled.

I saw my father rushing over to us, and I started to greet them both.

"Cari, this is my father..."

"Felix," Cari said as if all her breath had left her body.

Looking between them my eyes locked in my father's face. My father didn't look at all upset. He was now calm, and he looked confused.

"Yes, how did you know that?" I asked just as I saw Gravy enter the room.

"Because this is your mother, baby girl. Cari, how could you? After all these damn years this girl has gone through enough, and now you decided to step in?" he boomed, and it seemed as if the entire dining room was looking at us, including Gravy, Stephanie, and now Miracle who started her way over.

"My what?" I asked, looking at Cari.

She had my eyes and my nose. She really looked like an older me, and to be honest, time hadn't been nice to her. Questions ran through my mind looking at this woman, but mostly why she was sent here to me after running out of my life at birth.

"Fiona, I can explain. Felix, I have some explaining for you both. Come to my room, and we can talk," she said, and neither is us refused. Honestly, I wanted to rush out of this building and find somewhere to scream. Why did she come here? I was grown now, and I didn't need her at all.

We walked past Gravy, and he looked as if he needed me, but I couldn't stop following her. It was as if my body was under a spell and all I could do was whatever she asked. Entering her room, we both sat side by side while she sat across from us in a chair.

"When I had Fiona I was only twenty-three, remember Felix?" Cari asked, and my father nodded.

"Remember I had those nightmares the entire pregnancy, and I couldn't stop them. You had become so angry and tired, and it wasn't you, it was me. There has been something wrong with me for years, and I was too afraid to tell anyone. My mother Stevonia was a Russian witch," Cari continued, and my eyes grew. I thought back to when the witch said that I was just a powerful if not more than her.

"When I gave birth to my beautiful baby girl, Fiona my powers took over, and I spooked the doctors. Your father was late because of his work having him out of town. When he came to get you, I had left because they had called an insane asylum for me. I didn't know what to do or where to go with this, and a witch sought me out. She showed me how to control them and become the woman I am today. I am here to help you with yours," she said, and it was as if I finally found my voice.

"Bitch, are you on some type of dope? If I were a witch, you wouldn't be standing here for what you did to me. At the same time, I'm am so glad you got one night to enjoy what your baby girl became. I want you out first thing in the morning. Daddy, you can stay and entertain this woman if you want, but I will not. I have a party to plan," I said, getting up and leaving. When I got outside the door, I saw Miracle standing against the wall.

I sped past her ass too. I didn't have time for her tears or questions. I was walking so fast that I rushed into my office full speed walking right past Gravy and Joshua.

"Damn, you good?" Gravy asked, and it shook me a little.

"Sorry. Hey nephew! I have missed you sooo much!" I squealed, hugging Joshua so tight. He had a bruised eye, and it hurt me to have to ask. "What happened?" I asked, and he looked at Gravy.

"It got handled, but look, you ain't called your auntie on Serena, did you?" Gravy asked, and I knew it more to the questions from the other night.

"Why would I do that, Gravy? My auntie wouldn't just handle someone like that," I said, crossing my arms over my chest.

"Joshua, go hang with Auntie Stephanie until I get done with Jude," he said, and Josh walked to the door. I turned my camera on to make sure he found Stephanie, and when he did, I put my attention back on Gravy.

"They found Serena chopped up, but she had a string going through her body, and her body parts were sprawled all over the house on the string. They couldn't get in to get her down, and her teeth were found inside a doll," Gravy said, and I watched as his hairs on his neck rose. "That's not funny Jude, the fuck!" He pushed me back and moved around me, and I didn't notice I was actually smiling about it.

"I know Gravy, but you know I have nothing to do with that. I have been with you most of this time. I won't lie though. She deserved that shit. It seems like this year is the year for mothers to step back into their kids lives, huh?" I huffed, flopping into my desk chair. I grabbed a blunt and locked my door from my desk and sparked up as Gravy sat across from me.

"What you mean?" he asked.

"Cari is my mother. She and my father are currently talking in her room about everything. I don't know how to feel, so please don't ask. I swear I had nothing to do with Serena, and if I unknowingly did, I am sorry. So much is going on that I don't know where I have been and what's been going on," I said, taking a few long pulls.

"Damn Jude. You think your pops going to take her in?" he asked, looking concerned.

"I don't know, and I don't care. She will not get any alone time with me. I told Cari to be out of here in the morning." I put the blunt out and was about to walk out when Gravy grabbed me and pulled me onto his lap.

"You gotta forgive her if she means you well. At least hear her out about why she left." He said and smiled.

I kissed him hard and felt his dick getting hard. Before I knew it, he was fucking me on my desk, and my mind was not even focused. I couldn't tell Gravy about what my mother had said. Picture his reaction to the woman he fucking being a whole witch. This pussy would keep me from telling him that tonight. Everything else we will handle when we got there.

―――――

Once we were done, we went back to everyone else, and I found Joshua with Stephanie.

"Girl is everything okay?" she asked, and I shook my head no. I didn't see any reason to lie to Stephanie because she was my closes friend.

"We can talk tonight after the dinner. I just want to make the best of it," I said, and she nodded.

I could feel my parents enter the room. I looked right over and saw them walk in together smiling and laughing. My father looked so happy that it was heartwarming, but I still felt some type of way about Cari just coming back all of a sudden. I looked around for Miracle, and she was nowhere to be found. I decided to make tonight a good night either way and sat down with Joshua and Gravy to enjoy some fish and chips.

THE NEXT MORNING, I woke up to the sound of the news playing downstairs in my living room. It was odd because I know I didn't leave the TV on. Getting up, I grabbed my robe and gun and went to check it out. Going down my hallway, I could hear the new broadcaster saying that they had found the body of a woman two miles from my shelter. That piqued my interest because I didn't want that bad reputation coming from the news. That would scare people into coming for help, and I didn't want that. Getting to the top of my steps, I could see my mother sitting happily watching. Lowering my gun, I smacked my lips and hurried to stand dead in front of her.

"Cari, you can't just walk in here when you feel like it. This is my fucking home, not yours. You lost that privilege when you walked out of my life!" I said, and she simply smiled.

"You sound so much like me. You look just like me too. Sit down Fiona so that we can really talk," she said and motioned for me to sit. When she did, my body flew to the chair sitting itself down.

"Sorry didn't mean to throw you. I still got a little alcohol in my system." She smiled.

"What is there to talk about, Cari?" I asked, rolling my eyes. I was more upset with the fact that she was sitting in front of me than the fact that she was able to sit me down.

"You have been having blackouts and bad dreams, haven't you?" she asked me, and I rolled my eyes. I wasn't about to entertain this shit.

"When we came together, even now, your heart rate is beating a mile a minute, huh?" she asked, and she was right. It was beating so fast because I was seconds from jumping across this table.

"Why did you come back, Cari? I don't need you anymore! My father raised me never saying a bad word about you but never saying anything amazing either. I didn't know your name or what you looked like. I watched other girls' mothers come to get them from school and make their cupcakes for class while my mother was out living her best life. With all odds against me I still made it to do something great and amazing, but then you show up, and everything goes to shit?" I huffed I wanted to slap fire from her dizzy ass, but it wasn't worth it.

"Fiona, I came back because I now have control of my powers. When I gave birth to you, the powers had become out of control, and I marked you with a curse. This year on Halloween, all your judgments will be held in front of your face, and I wanted to protect you. I have traveled to world to find a way to break this curse, but the only way is for a true love's kiss on Halloween night." She said, and I felt like something was happening to me.

"Why should I believe anything you say, Cari?" I challenged.

"Because I am your mother and I have always wanted what was best for you even if it wasn't me! The birthmark that you have that is in the form of a crescent moon, which is a scar from the curse. You real birthmark is on your head like your father. Right above your neck." She smiled a little, and I touched that area. I always wondered why I had two, but I just felt special about it. The crescent moon was on my stomach and Gravy has asked about it, but I didn't want to make a big deal out of it. Either way, she was proving her point.

"Fiona, I never wanted to leave your side. When they told me that they were sending me away, I knew I would never have the chance to come back. I'll be damned if I looked at you grown all doped up, unable to see you grown and remember those moments, nah you mother wasn't going out like that."

I watched her get up and come over to me. I couldn't move or resist. She rubbed my face, and when I looked at my fingers, I saw flickers of electricity coming from the tips.

"You have powers Fiona, you just have to embrace them and accept them. I am not here to harm you at all. I just want to make sure you are okay," she said, and as she rubbed my face, I felt my tears fall. This was all I wanted from my mother, to be here when I felt at my lowest and to pick me up. This is what I craved for years, but for some reason, all of me wouldn't fall for her story.

My eyes shot open, and she was gone, no longer in my living room, and I was able to get up and move. When I looked at the TV, they had a picture of Miracle and a video beside it of officers carrying a body from the woods. I covered my mouth and looked around my house but didn't find my mother anywhere. I couldn't believe what I had seen or felt, but I could still feel my mother near.

Going to handle my personal hygiene and get dressed, I sped to the shelter to see if she was there. When I didn't find her there, I decided to calm down and get back to business as usual. I wouldn't let Cari take me off my square, and I need to get this party decorated today in preparation for tomorrow night. Getting straight to it, I blocked out any feelings of my mother and got to work.

"DADDY! JUICE PLEASE!" Joshua whined as we rode around the city. I heard my little man, but my mind was everywhere.

For some reason, I couldn't get Fiona's ass off my mind. Fiona was also entering my dreams, and this shit was crazy. I didn't know if this was what love was supposed to be like, but I was going crazy. I felt like I needed to be around her and inside her twenty-four/ seven.

"Okay, lil man but stop that damn whining," I said, getting a little stern.

Joshua was about to be three in two months, and he needed to start using his words and talking. Joshua knew how to talk, but he would only talk to Fiona and me. I watched his head fall into his chest and could see his big bottom lip poking out. I shook my head and trying to get my face right cause Joshua looked like a little me.

"Pick your head up, son. Never let anyone see it fall. You are a king and king's heads are always held high. Let's go inside this store and get you some juice," I said, pulling over to the corner store.

I got Joshua out the car, and we walked past some thugs on the corner. I was well known, but these weren't my niggas. I didn't care because I stayed strapped. We browsed through the store and Joshua chose and Jungle Juice, and I got a cold Pepsi, and we went to pay for it.

"That will be $3.69," Unk the store owner said.

I gave homie a five as two young boys walked over to Joshua with candy in their hands. I grabbed the bag and then Joshua, and we walked out of the store.

"I got the fire, man," a young boy said, and Joshua looked back.

"I'm straight," I said over my shoulder getting Joshua in the car seat.

"Nah, he don't fuck with us lil niggas no more. Nah Gravy is big time now," I heard as I clicked Joshua 's seat belt.

I looked up and saw Corey, a nigga me and Marco had crossed paths with a few times. He was salty because we got out, and when we did, the business went to him when shit got rough. Marco was never supposed to be in the game that long. He moved away from this shit but ended up right back in it.

"Corey." I nodded and kept going to my side of the car.

"Damn, it's like that? I'll catch you though," this fat nigga said, and I nodded. I smiled getting into my car and pulling off.

I find it so funny how when a nigga gets out the game and gets some business about himself, I mean some legit shit, niggas can't be happy for them. Corey had dreams, but he let the game become bigger than his dreams. I got out for my son, and I don't regret shit. Even though I was out of the game, Corey threat was heard, and I would still handle mine.

I had to get my things together for this party tomorrow night, and Joshua was going to be with his grandma. I really didn't feel like going because of all the shit that has been going on with Fiona, but I couldn't make myself not go. It was as if I had to be there. After dropping Joshua off at school, I found myself parked outside the witch's office. Something pulled me out of my car and to her door. As I went in, I heard her talking to someone, and they came into view it was Cari. I was quiet walking in but they both stopped, and Cari turned, and both their eyes were on me.

"We can finish this later." She smiled, winking at me. I didn't move.

"Gravy, or should I call you Gerald. That is your name isn't it?" the witch asked.

"How you know my name?" I asked.

"I've been around. Why don't you come service us?" she asked standing, and I couldn't lie I wanted to. I also felt myself pulling away, but my legs wouldn't stop moving toward them. I watched as Cari used her hands to lay me against the desk.

"My name is Amina. I want you to cater to our bodies first, and then you can have your treat." She climbed on me, and my dick was already at attention. I couldn't fight them as Amina slide down my dick.

"Mmmmmmm," she moaned, and I had to close my eyes.

This shit was mesmerizing. I don't know what Amina had between her legs, but she had me going crazy. I grabbed her hips as she rode me faster and faster. I was about to nut when she snapped her fingers and told me not to. The sensation stayed, but I couldn't cum. I was going crazy when Cari came covering my face with her pretty pink pussy. She smelled like honeydew and tasted just as sweet. I couldn't believe what was happening to me, but I couldn't lie and say it didn't feel amazing.

"Shit Gerald, eat this pussy baby!" Cari moaned, and my tongue was going so fast I didn't know where I had gotten the talent. Before long, Cari was cumming all over my face and Amina on my dick. They both jumped down and in unison got on their knees.

"We both want to share your juices!" Amina panted, and I stood to my feet. I jacked my dick until I was shooting what felt like buckets into Cari and Amina's faces. I watched as they licked the big load off their faces and then licked it off each other's face. I had to shake my head because this was some new shit, but the nut was well worth it.

"I hope we can get the same or even more tomorrow, Gravy," Amina said and snapped her fingers, and all of a sudden, we were all in the same position as before.

"What the hell?" I yelled, and Cari turned back to Amina. It was as if I had just walked in again. "The fuck kind of shit is this, yo?" I boomed.

"Don't worry. You are clean, and so are we. Thank you for your services, but you are no longer needed." Amina swiped her arm across the air, and I flew out of the office, and the door slammed shut and locked in my face. I banged on the door as people walked by looking at me as if I was crazy.

To be honest, I was starting to believe that I was crazy. Getting myself together, I hopped in my car and headed to pick up my costume to match Fiona. I didn't know if they did that shit to go back and tell her, but I would deny that shit until the cows came home that it wasn't me. It was two days until Halloween and shit was already getting crazy around here.

EVERYONE WAS HAVING a great night but me. I hadn't spoken to Gravy since the day before yesterday, and I was worried he wouldn't show up. My mother was here with my father, and they looked as happy as could be. I didn't know how my father was happy knowing Miracle was just killed but he was. At the same time, his eyes were off. I had looked at my father for twenty-six years, and his eyes were just off to me.

Maria has just texted me that she had gotten the shelter children to sleep finally and I was content until I felt a pair of hands on my shoulder. Turning around, I saw the best looking Captain Hook I could ask for.

"Miss Swan," Gravy said, and I burst into laughter. I had really fallen for his bug goofy ass, and I could finally admit that I loved him.

"I am the dark one actually but good job. Let's go." I pulled my finger by him, and he followed. I laughed at how he acted as if I was really pulling him to the dance floor. I had to admit we pulled off this Once Upon a Time theme. Stephanie and Kevon were dressed as Belle and Mr. Gold, and they were too cute as well.

Gravy didn't stand a chance with me on the dance floor, and I was giving him my all.

"Do it, baby girl!" I heard Cari say, and I felt Gravy back up a little making me fall back a little.

"You okay?" I asked him, and it was like a gust of wind took over, and everyone looked at the doors. The witch had made it in.

"Amina!" Gravy said louder than he expected, but his eyes were full of lust. I mushed him in the head and walked over to her.

"Thank you for finally showing up," I said, voice laced with attitude.

"Watch yourself, Fiona. I said you were more powerful, but even you haven't found this power yet. I had some loose end to tie up, and they are now handled. Now to trick the crowd, huh?" She smiled and started to walk to her section. People came over to get their palms read and meet her, and I watched in amazement as she read them. I felt something come over me and I had to go to my office.

I sat at my desk and tried to catch my breath. I was just about to light my blunt when Gravy stormed in like a raging bull.

"Fiona, why did you leave like that? What the fuck has been going on with you?" he boomed, and it felt like his voice shook the walls.

"If I'm fucking you, I would tell you, Gravy! Who the fuck are you to question what I do and where I go? Why are you up my ass?" I screamed, and he twisted his face up, but I kept my same stare.

"You on some other shit brah, spitting that hot shit! You witch bitches just stay the fuck away from me, ya hear me?" he yelled and pointed at me. I peered my eyes at him as he walked out.

"UGHHH!" I screamed, launching my glass bowl of candy across the room. I was heated, and I had never felt the rage I was currently feeling. Grabbing my car keys and purse, I ran out of the building and drove to the closest bar I could find.

⬤▭▭⬤

After a few shots I was feeling calmer, but I just needed to be dicked down. I tried to call Gravy but his ass didn't answer, and I wasn't about to blow his ass up. I took another shot and tried my best to get up from the bar. I was fucked up and laughing at my damn self, but my worries were all gone. I saw Corey, a fat nigga from back in the day, looking at me like I was his next meal. I smiled and started to hear these words in my head as we stared each other down. I began to say them and watched as he got up looking at me lustfully and followed me to my car.

I didn't know how we ended up at his house, but Corey was ripping my clothes off and his fat ass was making me feel good. I ain't going to lie. I thought after Marco that only skinny niggas were in, but these fat niggas be breaking backs in too.

"Damn Jude, you got a nigga hard as fuck," he groaned, kissing my neck. I felt him stick three of his fingers in me and I arched my back. "You gotta take this if you about to ride this monster," I heard him say, and the pain was easing.

Corey worked my pussy and then bit my neck, and I saw a flash. I was watching dogs tear Serena's body to shreds. Then back to Corey. I was horrified, but my body was focused on Corey. Pushing him back he fell on the floor, and I jumped on him.

The Patrón has a bitch nasty as fuck because I grabbed his huge dick and stuffed it in my ass. I was riding his big dick and didn't feel a thing. Another flash came, and I was cutting up Serena's remains and hanging them around her house. I smiled and rode him faster. I felt his fingers playing on my clit, and I was about to cum off just that. Another flash came as I looked over my work of Serena's body parts and teeth around her house.

"Shit Jude, a nigga is about to nut!" Corey yelled out, and I came back to reality. I wasn't drunk anymore. I was feeling everything happening, and I was back to me. I knew what I had to do.

I rode Corey harder and watched as he closed his eyes. I reached down and grabbed a knife that he had under the table. When the tape ripped his eyes shot open, but he was also cumming. As soon as he grabbed my hips and closed his eyes, I stopped and slit his throat. I got up and watched as he shook trying to cover the wound but it wouldn't work. I cracked my neck and felt the best I had ever felt.

Waving my hands over his body, I closed the wound and dressed him. I was amazed at how easily I had come into my powers with acceptance. Once he was dressed, I had his body walk itself into the street where a truck hit him. I smiled and walked to my car and pulled off.

"Your powers weren't supposed to start until Halloween night," I heard and felt my mother's presence.

"I guess you were given the wrong information. It seems like my powers have been active for a while," I said, parking in the side of the road and looking at my mother.

"I thought this was Amina's work. Fiona, you have to be careful with this. Did you curse Gravy?" she asked, and I just looked at her. I turned my head from side to side and smiled at her.

"Your fears will be the death of you woman." I pulled off, and she begged me to stop. I was feeling free and honestly the best I ever had. I didn't curse Gravy. I wouldn't have to.

"Fiona, I need to tell you something so stop!" Cari screamed, and the car immediately stopped.

I tried to make the car start again but for the life of me, it wouldn't. Focusing in the car, I tried to use my powers, but it was useless. Looking at Cari, I saw a vein sticking out of her forehead, and I knew she had control at this time. Frustrated threw my seat back to listen to her.

"You are so stubborn like Felix. Listen you need to watch Amina. You are still cursed, and with that, you can be controlled to do things you do not really want to do. You just killed a man for no reason!" she screamed, and I rolled my eyes.

"He wasn't the first," I said nonchalantly.

"Oh no! Excuse the hell out of me! You killed Serena too, but that woman deserved it!"

"Just like you, huh? I mean she just pulled a more recent act like you did to me, so why is she any worse than your ass?" I was amped up and had really heard enough.

"Fiona, one day you will see that what I did was for your own good. I have control now, and I will help you outlive this curse."

She vanished into thin air, and my car instantly started. I pulled off and headed back home. My head was starting to hurt and the closer I got home, the more it hurt. When I finally reached my bed, my body threw itself on my bed, and I was out like a light.

———

"Jude, you asleep?" I felt Gravy touch my back and trace my spine with his fingertips.

"Mmmmm," I moaned because it felt so nice. I didn't open my eyes though because not seeing him had a kind of mystery to it.

"Sorry for how I spoke to you earlier. I don't want to lose you. Can you forgive a nigga?" Gravy went on now massaging my ass. The shit felt so good that I was agreeing to any and everything.

"Can daddy work his pussy?" he said, and I felt his breath on my ass. He quickly pulled my ass into the air and told me to keep my head down. I was enjoying every minute because if it was one thing Gravy did well, it was eat some pussy.

SMACK!

Gravy slapped my ass so hard that I knew it would be red in the morning. When his dick all of a sudden entered me, I felt ice cold. I began to shiver, and I couldn't stop freezing. I was in agony as my toes froze and the ache crept up my body. I finally sat my head up and little, and while the feeling of Gravy was keeping me here, I almost died at the sight before me.

"Shit, you feel so fucking good, Jude!" Gravy moaned.

"I bet she do, nigga!" Marco boomed, and I kept my eyes on the corner of the room.

"WHAT THE FUCK?" Gravy yelled and jumped back grabbing me. I was frozen as I watched Marco come into the light.

He looked just as he did when he died minus the bullet wounds. Tears fell from my face as he neared us. Gravy pulled me behind him, and I was more worried for him than he should have been for me.

"This is what the fuck y'all do when a nigga die? Trust me, dog. She ain't worth shit! This grimy ass bitch killed my seed! Just wait Fiona, tomorrow night I will have my revenge, and you will burn for this shit!" He got closer and then vanished making me scream. Gravy walked over, got dressed, and then just looked at me.

"Fiona, what the fuck was that?" he asked, and I had to be honest. I told Gravy everything. How I killed Serena and Corey and possibly Miracle, but I didn't know yet. I couldn't remember killing Miracle, but I could now remember everything else. I put my hands on my head because it began to hurt again.

Gravy went to get me some water and then came back and sat across from me this time. It hurt, but I understood why he did it. I couldn't focus on that right now because I needed my head to stop hurting so that I could figure it what's really going on.

"Stop trying too hard and relax, Fiona. Once you focus, your migraine will instantly go away. You have to focus, baby girl." I heard my mother say and then she touched my shoulder calming me a little.

"What the fuck?" Gravy jumped back, but I had to focus.

For the first time I had taken my mother's advice, and it worked. I focused on my newest memory. When Cari touched me, I saw her giving birth to me and how her eyes lit up when she looked at me. I saw her touch my stomach and when she did, the curse began. I saw how the doctors looked at her and how she hurt when she left me in the room alone. Opening my eyes, she sat in front of me holding my face in her hands crying. I couldn't hold my tear either as I hugged her as tight as I could.

"Sorry I gave you such a hard time!" I voiced, but she told me to hush.

"It's is okay. Right now we need to get you and everyone you love somewhere safe," she said, and I grabbed my phone. I called

Stephanie, and she was going to meet us at the shelter since she and Kevon were still close. My father was already there, and we just needed to get there.

"So what the fuck was that in the bedroom, Fiona? Cari?" Gravy asked pacing the floor.

"That was part of her curse. If you plan to be in her life, then you need to accept this and come with us. You need to be holding my hand when I get us to the shelter," Cari said, reaching for Gravy. He looked at me, and I nodded my head, and he grabbed Cari's hand. In a flash, we were in my office.

"Now I have a protection spell on the shelter, but Amina is a powerful witch. She had been getting items to make her way in this entire time. I can't believe she got to you." Cari went off looking out the office windows.

"Amina, who is that?" I asked.

"The witch, from the party," Gravy said, sitting down as if he was going to be sick.

"How did you know that?" I asked Gravy because he wasn't even into this, and anytime he saw the witch he was with me. She never gave us her name.

"I told him her name at the party." Cari stepped in before he could answer. I looked at Gravy, and he turned his head. He was lying, and I knew it.

"Tomorrow anyone that you have harmed will come back to this world to get their revenge. If you live to the first of November, then you will be spared for the rest of your life. A true love's kiss can also break the spell, but that is rare."

My mother ran everything down to us, but I had zoned out. Everyone I had ever wronged would be a long list. My head began to hurt, and it felt like someone was knocking my shit in with a gravel. I tried to stand and get to my mini fridge for a water bottle and blacked out.

9 / GRAVY

I CARRIED Fiona to a room and laid her down. The past few events had scared me, and I needed to check in on Joshua. Calling my mother, she reassured me that he was doing just fine and that I didn't need to worry. It didn't help much, but I knew he was okay.

I watched as Fiona slept and wondered if this was at all worth it. Here I was trying to make this work, and I didn't know what I was trying to work out. Even though we were fucking, me and Fiona hadn't made anything official.

I didn't want to make her think that this is why I wanted out, but I mean his was some crazy shit. Witches and dead niggas coming back didn't happen in the hood, and the shit was far from my beliefs.

I pulled out a blunt and opened the windows. Lighting up, I thought about seeing Marco and how that shit had spooked my ass. The way he spoke to Fiona and how she never said a word also was sitting on my mind. How could she kill that nigga's seed if she was never pregnant? Fiona had some talking to do, but I could wait until she woke up and we handled this shit. I may have been wrong for fucking his bitch, but her killing his child was the ultimate wrong.

After smoking my blunt, I saw Fiona was still out. I decided to shower and find something else to put on. I started the shower nice and hot for a nigga. The bathroom became steamy so quick, but I didn't think anything of it. Stepping into the shower, I began to wash myself when I started to see Amina playing in her pretty pink pussy. My dick rocked up so quick thinking about her.

"Make me cum, Gravy! Please!" she moaned out so clear, and I thought I was tripping.

I felt hands caress my back and then something swallow my dick. I looked down, and Amina was sucking the soul out of my dick while playing in her pussy. The water had her hair soaked but then feeling of her mouth on my dick gave me an extra drive. I became hungry for her pussy. I wanted nothing else at the moment but to feel her and to control her emotions.

Lifting her, I slammed her against the shower wall and dug into her pussy. Amina dug her nails deep into my back, and I let out a groan. I was fucking the shit out of her ass, and I knew she was enjoying it the way her pussy was holding my dick hostage.

"This is what the fuck y'all need to keep y'all sane, huh?" I groaned, pumping in and out of her.

"Yessssss don't stop!" She screamed, and I didn't even care if Fiona ass heard us. I could feel Amina holding me back from cumming too quick, and the feeling was amazing.

"Fuck!" I groaned, slapping her ass while holding her with one arm.

"Give me your child!" She moaned, and I came long and hard inside her. I couldn't hold back.

I thought all my energy would be gone, but it was still hard as a rock and horny as hell.

"Now you have someone else to service." Amina got out the shower and pulled my wet body to the room. I saw Fiona still asleep in her bed, and I looked at Amina confused.

"Take her and give her your seed. NOW!" Amina demanded, and I couldn't control myself. I spread Fiona's legs and began to eat her pussy while Amina watched.

"Fuck, Gravy! Don't stop, baby!" she moaned, and I watched as she kept her eyes closed.

Amina sat in the chair beside the bed and spread her legs playing in her pussy yet again. Head bitches really never got tired, and I was all for the games.

"Now fuck her pussy Gerald," Amina demanded, and Fiona's eyes shot open.

She couldn't stop me because I was already deep in her guts fucking the shit out of her. As much as she wanted to refuse at first, I had Fiona cumming back to back, and I had yet to nut again.

"Gravy, what are you? Fuckkkk!" Fiona moaned, and I couldn't control myself. She felt so different but good. Fiona's nails dug into my skin, and I pounded her spot harder as her eyes roll into the back of her head. Amina got up and began to suck and bite Fiona's nipples, and Fiona's legs began to shake.

"She is ready, Gerald. Give her your everlasting seed now!" Amina's command had me dropping buckets into Fiona. Fiona's body shook for what felt like minutes, and then she passed back out.

"Good boy," Amina said, and I blacked out.

I began to come to feeling cold and wet. When I opened my eyes, I had the shock of my life as I was alone in the middle of the woods next to a dancing fire. I was chained to the tree stump, and it was raining like crazy.

"AMINA!" I yelled over and over until I couldn't anymore. I sat there defeated as it rained on a nigga. *Damn, this is what good pussy gets my ass.*

"COME ON, baby. We finally have some time to ourselves, so let's make the most of it," Kevon said, but I wasn't feeling it.

"Kevon, we been fucking since you got back home. Do not start with me. On top of that, you thought I didn't see you texting that bitch Aubri. Get the hell on. I'ma only be nice in public, but at home we not fucking with each other," I explained, getting my clothes from the closet we once shared.

Kevon was a hoe, and I didn't find out until I gave him the pussy. With everything going on, I didn't want to stay at the shelter and have any parts of it. Cari seemed afraid, but that bitch didn't know me, so I was good.

"Where are you going now?" Kevon asked, and I rolled my eyes.

"TO WASH MY ASS IS THAT OKAY?" I yelled, and he threw his hands up. I wasn't in the mood, and it was going on one o'clock in the morning. I hurried my ass into the bathroom and enjoyed my shower. My mind drifted off to Fiona when I heard a loud thud come from the room. When I heard shuffling and another thud, and things went silent, I turned my shower off.

"Kevon?" I yelled out, and I didn't hear anything. I grabbed my towel and dried off. Getting my clothes on, I was mad that I didn't bring my purse. Fiona never let me leave without my gun, but I left it downstairs in the couch in my purse.

When I was finally dressed, I stepped it the bathroom and was horrified when I saw Kevon's head spinning on some type of machine. I screamed to the top of my lungs while running to get my purse. When I got to the living room, I saw my front door was open. Going to shut it, I had my gun trained on the door. Anyone playing tonight would feel lame. Believe that!

"Oh, I'm not out there. I missed you, sweetness," I heard from behind me and the voice was familiar and still laced with venom. My body froze sew in its tracks.

"Don't be afraid now. You weren't afraid sixteen years ago," the voice said again. This time I turned to face him, and he looked just the same.

"LeRoy, ho-how did you come back?" I asked because I couldn't believe he was sitting in my house.

"How did I come back after you killed me? Oh, you can thank that pretty little Fiona for that," LeRoy said, standing to his feet. The room got cold as ice and LeRoy started towards me.

"You're dead. You can't be here. This is not fucking real." I closed my eyes.

"Oh, this is as real as I want this to be thanks to the curse," he said, and when I opened my eyes, I was laying in my back in my old bedroom. "This was our place right, sweetness. Let's relive our favorite moments," he said, and out of nowhere, he appeared on top of me. I tried to push him off, but I was back to my eight-year-old self. I felt him enter me and the pain was agonizing.

"Stop please, daddy!" I cried because it felt like barbwire was wrapped around his nasty little dick.

"We are far from done, sweetness," he groaned, and I screamed in pain.

I endured his rape for what felt like hours, and when I looked at my Hello Kitty clock, it had only been twenty minutes. Tears stained my face as he pounded inside me. I suddenly began to scream. I killed him, and he was not really here! He wouldn't have this power over me in death too.

"Get off me!" I screamed and grabbed a handful of his balls squeezing them until I felt a warm squishy liquid encase my palms.

"Ahhh shiiit! You little devil bitch!" he screamed and rolled off me. I grabbed my dolls and walked over to him bent over holding himself.

"You would know the devil when you saw it, huh?" I kicked him and stuck my doll up his ass feet first.

"Ahhhhhhh!" he yelled, and I smiled wickedly.

"Damn Daddy, you can only take three dolls?" I mocked, wiggling doll number four in his face.

"Stop!" he screamed, and the room began to come back to my real home.

He slowly disappeared, and I breathed heavily. The house was a mess, and it was now two thirty in the morning. I broke down crying thinking about my childhood and how I was so happy when I finally killed that man. LeRoy loves his liquor, and one night I had finally had enough when I put rat poison in his liquor. LeRoy guzzled the drink down as usual and never woke up again. I went into foster care after that, and I was perfectly fine with that. My foster mother didn't like me at first and thought I would be a burden until I became the breadwinner at fourteen.

I might have had a hard life, but I wouldn't let that shit define my life. I grabbed my keys and purse and headed for the shelter. This was some crazy ass shit, and I needed Fiona to explain what the fuck comes with this damn curse that everyone was talking about.

Pulling up to the shelter, it was dark. I walked right in and used my phone's flashlight to see.

"Stephanie?" I heard Maria yell out, and I waved my light. I found her and the children in the only lit room in the building.

"Hey, are you guys okay?" I asked hugging and speaking to Maria and the children. I looked over to make sure everyone was here, and they were, which relaxed me a little bit. Maria's face was bruised, and she was bleeding from the top of her head down her forehead.

"We are now. Things have been crazy tonight. My ex-husband came back to life and attacked the children and me. I killed him when I caught him trying to molest my youngest. We finally got away, but he is somewhere out there. We haven't seen him in a few minutes." Maria rambled in a shaky voice. Looking at the kids, everyone was terrified.

All of a sudden, the lights come back on, and we hear Fiona calling out for Maria. When we open the door, we are all shocked to see that it's morning and everything is up in operation.

"Stephanie, what just happened?" Maria asked me, and I wasn't so sure. I looked around, and we were all in clean clothes and looked ready to start our shifts.

"What y'all doing in there? Girl, anyway last night was lit! Kevon is in your office he wanted to see if you were okay," Fiona said and winked at me. I couldn't fix my face to seem okay. Last night was very real for me, and she wanted me to fake it.

"Maria, take the kids to their rooms and let them enjoy their day. I will figure out what happens and fill you in later," I said, turning to Maria and the kids with a warm smile.

Maria returned the smile and followed my orders. I pushed past Fiona, and she pulled me to the side.

"What is your problem?" She was acting clueless, and I just shook my head.

"Bitch, act like you had a normal night and I swear I will burn this bitch down! Last night was a nightmare, and we just pop up, and it's morning! I had just found all of them battered and scared for their lives because a man was chasing and attacking them, not to fucking mention, me seeing my dead father and the things that he was able to do! This takes the cake, so unless you want to explain, I have nothing to say to you!" I stood there as she let her head fall. I knew she would fold on me and that shit hurt.

"I'll follow you to your office," Fiona said, and we did just that.

When I walked into my office and saw Kevon, I was so happy and excited I jumped on him.

"Baby, what the fuck?" Kevon said, and I couldn't even speak. I was so happy to see him that I began to kiss him all over his face.

"I figured this could be a good start for forgiveness. He already knows, and I was going to tell you when I found you as well," Fiona started, and she told me everything. I sat back I my chair in shock as Kevon rubbed my shoulders.

"So, you can cast spells and make shit grow like weed, bitch?" I asked, and Fiona smiled with tears falling from her eyes.

"I mean maybe I have tried!" She laughed, and I got up to hug her.

"So what the fuck do we need to do? That shit last night was too real, and I can't go back through that today," I said honestly.

"You won't have to. I have my mother working on a spell that will alter the curse for my lives ones. I can protect myself," Fiona said, getting up to leave.

"Jude, you have my help regardless. Thank you for your honesty because bitch I was ready to let your ass go. I'm here with you, so don't leave me out the loop okay?" I said, and she smiled and hugged me. I felt Kevon touch my shoulder again, and she left the office.

"So, can I get some pussy now?" he said, kissing my neck.

"Nigga, back from the dead or not, you still fucking with that bitch so no! I am happy you're back though!" I said, kissing Kevon on the cheek and getting to work. I got on my computer and looked up as much information about witchcraft as I could, and the shit was demonic. I was scared just looking at the shit and hurried off. Kevon left soon after, and I printed what I could off and went to find Fiona.

When I got to her office, Cari opened the door. She looked as if she was expecting someone else, but she smiled and let me in.

"Have you seen Fiona?" I asked, and Cari shook her head.

"She said she had something to handle. Listen, I need you to stay here and Kevon as well," Cari said, and I told myself to just listen. All hell broke loose the last time I did my own thing, so I called Kevon, but he wouldn't answer. I kept trying, and on the last call, it picked up.

"Stephanie, you're too late. Kevon had a heart of gold," I heard Amina the witch say, and Cari had to have felt her on the phone because she asked me to hit speaker.

"What have you done, Amina?" I asked calmly.

"Wanna see what I've done, huh?" she asked excitedly.

Out of nowhere, Fiona's TV flashed on. There sat a man with his head covered and everything in me knew that it was Kevon. I saw Amina walk in with the phone in her hand as she revealed his face. Kevon looked terrified, and I squeezed the phone.

"Let him go, Amina!" I begged, and she smiled into the camera.

"I don't need to kill him if your friend and her mother don't make that potion. See, I only need his heart to make a potion of my own against theirs. If they don't make it, then he doesn't die," she said, and I looked at Cari.

"Cari..." I begged with tears in my eyes.

"Stephanie, we can't risk this! I am so sorry, but I can't risk Fiona like this," she said, and I looked at the screen.

"She has made her choice for you, Stephanie," Amina said and slit Kevon's throat. I cried and squeezed the phone as I watched his body shake in the chair. The TV went out, and I broke down, dropping the phone.

"I'm so sorry, Kevon. How could I let him go so easily again!" I screamed, and Cari came over and touched me.

"You did this for Fiona, and she will forever be grateful. I am so sorry, Stephanie. I know you have done so much already for Fiona, and this will be a hard pill to swallow, but you will have us to help you along the way," Cari said, and she helped me to the couch.

I sat there silently crying as Cari worked on her potion. Even though Kevon and I weren't in the greatest place in our relationship, I hoped he would forgive me, and I hope today went by as fast as it could. I was terrified for what was to come. This wasn't some normal hood shit.

11 / CARI JUDE

As my potion cooked, I heard slight snores coming from Stephanie. I was glad she finally got some rest because I could see her going crazy by herself. I knew this would be a lot for everyone to take in, and I couldn't help but feel responsible. I knew long before having Fiona about my powers, but I didn't want to accept them.

I had met Amina when I was in college, and she changed my life. She showed me where I was from and my ancestors. We also had some wild nights together, and I fell for her. Amina had to go away and never returned, and I was hurt. I was lost more than anything because I didn't know where to go from here or even if I belonged. That's when Felix stepped in and made me forget all about Amina for some time.

Felix Jude had a way with his hands and his words. Amina was a faint memory until I got six months into my pregnancy. Amina cursed Fiona before birth, and when I tried to remove it, I made it worse. I drunk a potion to make sure Fiona didn't have to go this alone, but I never knew that she would find so many people to care for her. I didn't have that with my gift, but Felix had given her a normal life, so she knew nothing about her gift until now.

Thinking about Felix, I went to check in on him because I hadn't since I was so focused on this potion. Looking at Fiona's desk clock, I saw it was close to one in the afternoon already. I was happy the day was going by fast, but that only meant night was soon approaching and things would get worse.

Slipping out of Fiona's office quietly, I walked down the hall to my room. Entering I didn't see or hear Felix on the bed where I had left him.

"You killed Miracle, didn't you?" Felix said from behind me, scaring me and making me step into the room. Felix looked deranged, and I didn't know where this was coming from.

"What... where did you come from?" I asked, and he stepped closer to me.

"I saw it, Cari! You sitting here lying, but I saw you kill her! Why would you do that if I came back to you willingly? That girl had a whole life to live, and you ruined it, why?" he asked now with his hands around my throat.

I couldn't respond if I wanted to because Felix was choking the life out of me. I retired to pry his hands from around my throat, but it was no use. I felt myself slipping from life, and he finally let me go.

"I...don't... understand," I coughed but was able to get out.

"I saw how you killed her on the TV. I just came on when I woke up. I went to find you and couldn't. I don't understand either, Cari. I never bad mouthed you to anyone. Miracle was innocent, and you killed her!" Felix's voice grew louder, and I tried to calm him down.

"Baby, I didn't kill her!" I finally yelled in my defense, and the TV came back on.

I watched dreadfully as my body walked over to Miracle looking lost in the woods. It seemed like the same place where Amina had killed Kevon, and I shook my head. I didn't even give the girl a chance as I stabbed her numerous times and watched her body fall. I stared at her struggling for air and then the TV went off.

"That wasn't you, Cari? You going to keep lying to me?" Felix asked, storming over to me. I backed up because I didn't want to hurt Felix. I needed him to calm down so that we could talk because I didn't remember any of this.

"Felix, you have to believe me! That wasn't me!" I screamed, and he wrapped his hands around my throat again. This time wasn't so pleasant as I pushed him back with so much force he fell back onto the table. "Oh my gosh!" I cried and ran to his limp body.

I shook him, but he wouldn't come to. I felt a small pulse and breathed a sigh of relief. Saying a healing spell, I got him, better but in a coma so that he wouldn't be able to attack me.

"Cari, why don't you come out of that protection spell and come play." I heard Amina's voice and saw her on the TV.

"You spiteful bitch!" I yelled and walked out of the room.

"Just come find me. We can make up for lost times." I could still hear her, but I didn't see her. I was growing angry, but I couldn't let her make me react. Fiona still needed me, and this was just a ploy.

"We will be waiting," was the last thing I heard as I placed my hand on Fiona's office door.

I immediately stopped and thought about the 'we' part of her last comment. When I walked in and saw Stephanie still asleep, I calmed down. Amina would feel me if it was the last thing I did.

I took Fiona's office phone and tried to call her, but she didn't pick up. Closing my eyes and focusing, I felt her presence and that she was okay. I went back to the potion and began back to mixing it together. It was almost done and in just enough time.

I had let me family down one too many times in my lifetime, and I wouldn't be doing that ever again. I would protect my family at all cost from Amina and her hurt ways. What we did in the past is between us and for her to bring my family into it shows she is not over it. I refused to let her win though. As many good times as we had, I couldn't redeem her from the hurt she has brought to my baby girl.

Fiona was perfect, and I couldn't ask for a better daughter. Since

I missed her growing up, I didn't have any credit to take for her blossom. I would forever be grateful for Felix stepping up though. Finishing up my potion, I looked over at Stephanie and saw her stirring from her sleep. I couldn't wait for all of this shit to be over so that I could start fresh with Fiona and get to know everyone who lived and cared for her as much as I did.

I walked into my home, and it was still ice cold. The past few weeks had been crazy, but it was nothing compared to what was going on today. With everything going on, I had put Marco to the back of my mind but seeing him and feeling him now had him front and center. I knew he was still here, and after catching Gravy and me, I knew he was upset.

I sat on my couch and decided to let Marco come to me. I felt so bad about the abortion, but I knew I couldn't take care of a child on my own at that time. Marco would just have to understand that and forgive me. Either way, he was leaving tonight.

"So you finally came to face me, huh Belle?" I heard him call me by his pet name.

"I'm not facing anything because you aren't here. You left me!" I said, and my volume elevated. I felt myself getting upset, and I couldn't help it. I didn't know how upset I was with Marco until now. Yeah, I aborted our child, but he left me no choice!

"You will always play the blame game Belle, and that's not how I saw you. This isn't on me!" Marco showed himself, and he carried a baby girl. She was chunky and looked just like him.

My eyes swell with tears, and I quickly wipe them, and I could see the anger in Marco's face.

"She is beautiful," I mustered up.

"While you out here shaming your mother, you ain't no better, Fiona. You aborted our child because you were afraid. She deserved a chance, and you held that from her. Now, look at you, fucking a right hand nigga though, Fiona! That shit is low, and that makes you a nasty dirty bitch," he said, and the baby vanished. Marco walked towards me, and I held my hands out to stop him.

"No! I will not be the only one to blame! Yes, I made some fucked up choices, but so did you, which landed you into that casket! I thought you were out of the game, Marco? Don't screw up your face now nigga! You want to yell that I did this shit because I was afraid. Well, you damn right I was afraid for myself and our child! What if they came back for us both? No child deserves that! All because her daddy couldn't stay out of the game!" I huffed, and I knew I was red. Marco stepped back, and his face was still.

My chest was raising so high that I had to sit down. I wasn't afraid of Marco, but I wanted him to know that I was hurt too! I didn't do anything to hurt him, and he needed to hear that. When Gravy exposed the information about Marco being in the game again, I was irate! I was more hurt than anything though, and Marco didn't give two fucks about that!

"Gravy though, Fiona?" he asked, and I looked up at him like he was crazy.

"Would some random dick be better for you? Who would you like to be fuck your girl while you're bug food? Help me understand, Marco!" I yelled, and the room shook.

"You better calm your ass down before I finish what I came for!" he said, walking towards me, but I didn't give a fuck.

"Do what you gotta do Marco, but I will defend myself!" I yelled, and he lunged at me, grabbing me by the shirt. I tried to use my power on him, but they wouldn't do a thing.

"Sabrina has lost her powers," Marco whispered in my ear. He twisted my arms behind my back, and I screamed out in pain.

Marco tore my shirt from my body and used it to tie my hands together. He threw my body on the couch and began to pace the floor looking at me lustfully. Marco stopped and came and ripped my skirt and panties off. I looked back because I couldn't believe what was about to happen.

"The least I can do is get this pussy before I kill you off," Marco said and shoved his dick deep inside my mouth. Marco aggressively fucked my face, and the shit was killing me. I was throwing up everywhere, but that didn't stop him.

Marco roughly pushed my head off his dick, and I fell to the ground, coughing my lungs up. I continued to throw my insides up, and Marco just walked around me grilling the fuck out of me. I wanted to reason with him, but my throat hurt too much to say a word. Marco walked towards me, and I held my hand up in my defense, and he stopped. Marco looked at my hand and spat something green and nasty on my face. At this point I had it. Marco was upset I get it, but I wasn't the only one in the wrong. Standing to my feet, I slapped the fuck out of Marco, and his face changed for a moment.

"You have lost your mind! Marco, I gave you the best of me for years and now because of ONE mistake you coming back to hurt me? You low down dirty bastard!" I screamed, and he backed up a little. I was pissed, and I was done holding back.

"Marco, I have done some really fucked up things but nothing to deserve this shit! Yes, I aborted your child, and I can't keep apologizing for this! It was not fair, and I know this now! Gravy has been here for me more than you know. Dealing with your fucking death took a toll on a lot of people. This has to stop!" I yelled, and he showed no emotion. I wasn't about to keep trying to read him though, and Marco knew that. I stood my ground as he looked me over. Out of nowhere, he disappeared. I looked around the house for a few moments and didn't see him anywhere.

"I'm sorry, Belle," I heard from behind me in a sincere voice, and then my body was bent over, and his dick inserted my vagina from behind while his thumb fucked my ass hole.

To make matters worse, I was fucking Marco dead ass right back. Marco might have been the living dead right now, but his dick game was still bomb! I felt his cold hands trace my spine and for some reason, his cold touch made me cum all over his dick.

This was some out of this world shit, but it felt too good for me to make him stop. Marco grunted and pumped inside my pussy with so much force. I didn't care because I was matching his thrust.

"This will always be my pussy, Belle. In life and in death," he grunted and began to shake behind me. Marco pulled out and fell back on the couch. I sat there spent because I haven't been fucked that good in years. I needed this shit more than Marco knew.

"Fiona, this shit hurts man, but I know that you're right. I can't lie. You have been through hell with me and always held it down. I still believe that you would have been a bomb ass mother though, Belle," Marco said, and I got myself together and sat on the coffee table. I was still recovering, and my pussy was so sore but hearing Marco say that made me want to talk.

"Marco, why would you feel any different?" I asked honestly.

"Seeing you with Gravy made me feel like this is what y'all had been plotting. I know he has been there, but I don't like that shit one bit, Fiona," he said, and I could see the anger in his eyes but more pain than anything.

"I didn't do this to hurt you Marco, but it really just happened. I will say that this is the happiest I have been since you were here with me," I said honestly, and Marco looked into my eyes.

"If you are happy then I am good. Just be careful, Fiona. I know you love me and carry a nigga in your heart. Just know I will always be with you, Belle," he said, and I got up to kiss him.

When I got to Marco's face, he dissolved into thin air. I felt the tears falling, but this time I was smiling. I knew he was saying that he forgave me and that was all I needed to hear. I battled with my decision the get the abortion every day, but I know I did what was best for me and at the end of the day that child. I wasn't ready, and no child deserved to watch me struggle.

Taking a deep breath, I walked to my bathroom and took a long hot shower. The hot steamy shower felt so good that I didn't want to step out. When I got it, I looked at my phone and saw that I had been in the shower for an hour. I couldn't believe it because my water didn't stay hot that long ever! Shaking it off, I stepped out of the bathroom and was met by a blunt object to the face.

"Fuck!" I screamed as my towel fell and my hand went straight to my face. My slippery nose let me know someone broke my shit.

"Oh, we ain't done, bitch!" I heard Corey and felt his hand wrap around my throat.

"Let me get my hands on that, bitch!" I heard Serena, and she came and punched me dead in the face as I struggled to get Corey from around my throat.

I was scared for my life as I felt the breath leaving my body. Out of nowhere, I touched Corey on the face, and he dropped me screaming out in agony.

"What the fuck, nigga?" Serena yelled grabbing me by the hair. I kicked her and ran back to my living room.

Serena met me at the front door with a smirk on her face.

"You won't get rid of me that easy," she said, and I stopped dead in my tracks.

"I don't plan to. I want you to suffer again!" I yelled, and Serena charged at me.

We tussled and then she stabbed me in the arm with something. The pain was excruciating, I didn't know what I did to kill Corey, but I couldn't get my powers to help me against her. Yet Serena was able to morph all types of weapons. I quickly ducked as she swung the knife again at me. I kept backing up when I saw a picture of Joshua on the wall beside me. Grabbing it, I thought of all the pain she would cause him one day and how she left him to die on the front porch. I looked, and she stopped dead in her tracks.

"Wha.." Serena started, and I smiled.

"He just needed you love, and that was too much, huh?" I asked, walking around her as she winced.

"What are you doing to me, Fiona?" she moaned, and I smiled harder letting a slight snicker out.

Serena's body was melting from the outside in. There was nothing she could do, and I owed this spell to my mother.

Once Serena's eyelids fell off her face, I backed out of the house and ran to my car. I didn't have my phone, and I didn't know what was going on at the shelter, but I prayed everyone was okay. I went to start my car, but it wouldn't start. I felt something hit my car and looked up to see Amina standing at the hood of my car.

"Gravy needs to be saved. Can you save this one, Fiona?" She smiled a sinister smile and disappeared through the night. I just couldn't win for losing.

Starting my car, I headed to the shelter to find my mother and to ask for her help. I knew Stephanie was also probably giving her a hard time, and I hoped she hadn't killed my best friend. This night was really getting worse, and I didn't know how much more I could take. This curse was an ultimate loss already it felt like.

I WAS ALMOST at the shelter when I felt a huge jerk in my wheel in my car. I threw my hand up as the car drove itself and passed my exit to get to the shelter. I knew this was nothing but Amina and she was trying to keep me away from my mother. I knew what I had to do to defeat her, and she wouldn't even see it coming.

My car took me into the woods, and we came up to a fire where I saw Gravy chained to a tree stump. When the car came to a stop, I hurried out and tried to get to him. Gravy had blood dripping from his mouth, and he was going in and out until I got to him.

"Jude, fuck going on, ma?" he slurred, and I could feel the anger rising in me.

"Just what I wanted," I heard Amina behind me. I got up and turned to her, and she was dressed in a white robe with no shoes. My mother walked out of the woods, and her eyes were all black. She looked dull and showed no emotion, and I shook my head. How did Amina get my mother?

"Why are you doing this to my family, Amina? What have I ever done to you?" I asked, and she laughed, but it seemed to echo around the woods.

"You are a product of me, and I could never gain access to you.

Felix knew it, and so did Cari. That is why they moved you away, and I couldn't reach you. It took me years, but I found you, and when Felix found out, he moved you again. You belong to me Fiona, and your life will give me the power that I need to make me and your mother whole again," she spoke, and none of it made sense.

"You are batshit crazy, Amina! All of this because you feel like you own me. This is not how life works Amina!" I yelled, and she walked towards me.

"Oh, I don't need your life," she said, and Amina quickly appeared between Gravy and me. "His will do," she said and grabbed his head.

I grabbed her hand and watched her bolt back and grab where I had touched her.

"I am not afraid of you, Amina!" I yelled, using my powers to uproot a tree and slung her across the forest.

I went to Gravy and tried to free him from the chains, but I felt myself being pulled back. Looking up, I saw my mother. I still in a daze by pulling me to the fire. I kicked and screamed for her to stop, but she got closer and closer. This time when I touched her, a white light grew from my palms. My mother fell to the ground letting me go and began to shake her head.

"What did I do?" she screamed, scooting away from me.

"We can discuss that later, Cari. Right now we have Amina to worry about," I said and was pushed by force against the tree. It felt as if my back had cracked and the pain was horrible. I felt it healing and knew my mother was working.

"Grab my hand. Together we are about to kill this bitch off." My mother reached her hand out, and I grabbed it. I felt the love run through my body as she pulled me to my feet. Together we built a light so bright that Amina had to raise her arm from the brightness. I could feel the power going through my body, and it was an out of this world experience.

A beam of our light rayed onto Amina, and I watched as she jerked and fell to the ground. Amina continued to jerk until her eyes rolled to the back of her head. My mother quickly let go of my hand, and I ran back over to Gravy. I used my powers to heal him, and he looked behind me with huge eyes. Looking back, I saw why he was looking that way. Cari stood over Amina's body and stared at her.

"Cari?" I asked, but she continued to look at her with such hate in her eyes.

Cari dug her hand into Amina's chest, and I saw her body fly up, and Amina's eyes shot open in a shocked expression. Cari ripped out Amina's heart, and Amina fell back to the ground dead. I let out a sigh of relief until I saw Cari began to eat Amina's heart.

"What the fuck, Cari?" I screamed, and she looked over at me.

"Her blood is rich and will give me more powers than I could ever imagine," Cari responded, and I threw up right then and there.

I couldn't see her eating the heart anymore, but I could hear her, and the thoughts made their own vision in my head as I threw up over and over. I felt a hand on my shoulder, and it was Cari. Gravy got up and stood far away from us, and I could see that Cari wanted me to go talk to him.

"Nah, stay right there," Gravy said with his hands out as I tried to walk over to him.

"Gravy, we are fine now. Amina is dead and is never coming back. We can go back to normal again," I tried to convince Gravy, but he didn't seem to be falling for it.

"Fiona, you are fucking crazy if you think we can just go back to normal after tonight! I was in death's door just now! You bitches think you can snap your fingers and things will be forgotten?" Gravy boomed, and I looked back at my mother, and she smiled.

"Maybe. Gravy shit was crazy, but the one thing I did do was keep your son safe. Through all of this, the one thing I did see is how much I love you and want to be with you. Yeah, I was cursed, and I outlived it. I can take the memories away if you really want me to. I love you Gerald and nothing, and no one can change that," I said honestly and began to walk towards him.

"Where is Joshua?" Gravy asked as I reached him.

"With your mother sleeping off his candy rush from earlier. I wouldn't let any harm come to him, and that is on my life. I love you both too much for that. I promise to figure out how to control this shit for you too, baby," I said, looking into his eyes. I loved this man, and he needed to know that before I made these changes to his memory.

"Can she control this shit, man?" He looked over me at Cari, and she nodded.

"You eating any more hearts after this shit, yo?" Gravy asked, and I burst out laughing.

"That was to make sure she never surfaced again. With Amina's heart resting inside of me, her powers are now under my full control. I can assure you that I will be working with Fiona with her powers and until then she can live with me if you feel safer that way," Cari said, and I looked back at Gravy. His eyes were locked on me, and I could tell he was battling with himself on this.

"Fiona, I can't lie. This shit ain't helping at all. The only thing calling for you is my heart and that shit loud as fuck. My son adores you, and I don't know how to tell him that you won't be in his life anymore," Gravy said, and I felt the tears coming. There was no controlling them as they made their grand entrance into our space.

"I understand," was all I could say. I was beyond hurt, and I didn't want to embarrass myself any further. I really thought that what we had before this would trump anything that has happened and that made me the fool.

"I don't have to tell my son that though. You are going to get your-self together and control your powers. Until then you need to be with your mom but still intensely involved for the shelter. They deserve to continue to have you there even with this going on. I love you too Jude, but the day I feel you fucking with my head, I swear I'll body your ass." Gravy mugged me and walked past me.

I smiled a little when I turned and saw him standing there with his arm out. Walking over to Gravy and into his arms, I felt so safe and as if we were the only two there. I broke down, and it was short lived. Lifting my head with his fingers, Gravy kissed me passionately.

The kiss was everything I needed, and I was enjoying every minute until I felt a burning sensation on my lower stomach.

Pushing my body away from Gravy, I grabbed my stomach and Cari rushed over to us. I lifted my shirt and saw my birthmark lighting up, but the shit hurt so fucking bad.

"What is thissss?" I screamed as Gravy tried to calm me down.

"The curse is leaving you, baby. Just wait, and the pain will subside," Cari said, rubbing her hand over the mark. Just as she said, the pain slowly went away, and I was feeling a little better.

Cari zapped is back to the shelter and went to check in Stephanie. I rode with Gravy to get Joshua, and we both headed back to the shelter. Once we got back, we had a huge breakfast prepared for the residents, and once they were all fed, we all met up in my office. I looked around and noticed that daddy wasn't there and neither was my mother.

"Stephanie, have you seen my parents?" I asked, and she shook her head no.

Looking at the cameras, I didn't see either of them. My office door opened the in walked both of them with suitcases in their hands and smiles on their faces. I was confused because I was going to have a talk with everyone, but I guess he had other plans.

"What's going on?" I asked, and Cari smiled walking over to me.

"You father wants to move in together, and I think it's time I did. These past few years have been depressing being away from him as well. I hope this is okay with you," Cari said.

"As long as you aren't late for dinner then I'm cool with it." I smiled and hugged her. I was ready to get to know Cari as my mother and not only a witch to help me with my powers. I wanted to give her a fair chance at being my mother for however long I had her.

"Alright, as you all know last night was crazy. I just want to thank you all for being here for me. I have gained a mother that I always wanted. From this day forward I want to build with you guys and if nothing else, last night really proved you guys' loyalty. Stephanie, I wanted to give you something that I never thought I could," I said and walked over to the door. Opening the door, Kevon walked in, and Stephanie jumped up. Stephanie stepped back as he greeted her and we all stepped out to let them talk. I watched everyone smiling as we walked to our cars and was grateful for the life I had. Last night was down right scary, but I could wait to see what was next for my family and me.

Fiona Jude

Two Years Later

"NiShon and Niveon, if y'all don't sit down somewhere!" I yelled in the dining room as my twins tore up the table set up that I had just fixed. In the past two years, I had given birth to twins, and they were working their way towards their terrible twos.

"They do not listen, momma," Joshua said and put his attention back into his iPad, and I shook my head.

"Don't I know it. When you father gets here, he will handle them legs though," I said, lying right through my teeth. The twins chilled out then and both tried to get into the same chair to sit down. I couldn't believe I was blessed with them both, but I wished it was a happy memory.

Since having the boys, Gravy believed that they weren't his. I had been grown tired of trying to explain that shit, and I was not about to change my mind.

NiShon was Gravy's twin all the way, but Nivieon looked just like Marco. It had been that way since birth, but I didn't think that it should have changed how Gravy treated us. I never told Gravy about what all happened that night, and when he changed his mind about having the thoughts erased, I did as he asked and never touched him or his memories. I felt like that part wasn't a part of his memory and didn't need to be. I did wonder how Nivieon came out looking just like Marco, but I didn't want to question my blessings.

"Why do y'all fight all the time, mommy?" Joshua asked, setting his iPad down and walking over to me. As much as I wanted to ignore his question, I never had and never will.

"Because sometimes we disagree on things like you and I. Remember when you wanted to buy that game on your tablet, and I said no. You were so upset with me that you didn't look at me for two whole hours. This is the same thing," I said, and he looked to be thinking about what I was saying.

"So that's why you and my brothers moved away?" he asked, and I nodded. That was all I could do because since moving, Joshua had never asked me why I left. As much as I wanted to take Joshua with me, I knew Gravy wasn't having that. Joshua was his life, and I knew he would kill me for him and not think twice about it.

"Somewhat yes, I don't want to keep talking about negative things. What do you want to do for Halloween?" I asked, and Joshua jumped for joy.

"Spider-Man!" he yelled, and the twins jumped up and down with him.

"Again? Ugh, why can't we do something like The Black Panther?" I tried to change Joshua's mind, but that was not happening.

"He wants to be Spider-Man, so let him!" Gravy's voice boomed around the dining room, and I rolled my eyes. The kids all ran towards him, and I watched as he picked NiShon up and left Joshua and Nivieon at his feet.

"Why are you here so early? I wasn't expecting you until later this evening for dinner." I continued setting up the tables and didn't hear Gravy's respond, so I looked up. He sat there with an opened envelope in his hand, and I looked at him confused as hell.

"I should have told you about this a long time ago, but I didn't have time for your mouth. I needed to know, and now that I do I feel a lot better." Gravy said and walked over handing me the papers out of the envelope.

Reading over the papers, I could see that Gravy had gotten the boys tested against my will. I was livid before I saw what they read.

As I already know, NiShon was Gravy's son, but Nivieon was not. I looked up, and Gravy's face didn't read a thing.

"See, I knew if you knew you would try and change them results, but it is what it is, man. I went by Marcos grave and spoke with my nigga, and I really think that my past behavior was uncalled for. I have this beautiful family, and I want to do whatever I have to keep this family. Nivieon isn't my son, but when the time comes, we can discuss that. I need you in my life, Fiona." Gravy dropped to one knee with a huge ring in a box. The twins and Joshua all cheered for joy along with some of the residents that lingered around the dining room.

"I'm sorry, but I need you to stand up Gerald," I said, and I watched his face switch all the way up, but I didn't give two fucks. I let Marco do this exact thing, and I wouldn't ignore my lesson.

"I care about you Gravy I do, and I mean that from the bottom of my heart. When I say something I mean that shit, and it's never to be questioned. I got my whole life together to make you trust me around your son again. When you found out I was pregnant, I felt that you were overjoyed but concerned as well. After they were born, you changed, and after seeing Nivieon, you really changed. I never asked you to change how you felt and would have gladly agreed to a paternity test. You canceled my choice in the whole matter. That had to be the most selfish thing that you have ever done to me, and I don't know how you can sit here and ask for my hand in marriage. I haven't spoken to you about us in months. You got your results, and now I'm supposed to just marry you, Gravy?" I asked, and I was seriously waiting for his answer. I was happy he wanted to marry me, but I didn't understand why.

The past few months have been hell without him, and I found myself using potions to be happy at times. I was just coming back to myself, and here he goes with his chubby ass making me want to change my mind.

"Fiona, come on man. I know you have some shit you ain't proud of that you want to be forgiven for," he said, and I wanted to slap the shit out of him.

"Obviously I do," I said looking him up and down, and his eyes narrowed. I knew that pissed him off, but I didn't give two fucks.

"Bet," he said and grabbed my arm.

"Stephanie, watch the boys," he ordered, and they all ran around while he dragged me to my office by the arm.

"The fuck is wrong with you?" I yelled ready for whatever.

"Fiona, you forgot who ran things here. I know I fucked up and me coming here was to make things right. I don't want to lose you to figure out where I want to be. I know where my heart wants to be and so do you. I won't hurt you again, and I promise you that. Now come here and bend that ass over." Gravy said, but I didn't move a muscle. I didn't give a fuck about his little speech. He wasn't getting no ass.

Gravy walked over to me and threw me against the wall. I was about to push him when he turned me again and placed my hands against the wall so that I couldn't do anything. I smiled slightly because Gravy knew I would shock him if I needed to.

Gravy bit my neck and pulled my pants down and smacked my ass so hard I knew that shit would bruise. I felt Gravy tear my panties from my body and ease his fingers into my pussy. Gravy played with my clit, and I can't lie I was enjoying every second of it.

"Tell me this is my pussy, Fiona," Gravy demanded into my ear, and it sent a tingle up my spine, but I couldn't say shit. Gravy stuck two fingers into me and began to pump them in and out, so I matched his finger thrust. I needed a good nut because fucking myself was nothing like having Gravy between my legs.

"You wanna play, huh." Gravy unzipped his pants and shoved himself all the way inside me. I scratched at the wall as he tormented my spot, and I couldn't get away. It felt like I was having back to back orgasms as my legs shook, but I was stuck to the wall.

"Shit! I bet that ass wishes she bent over like I asked now!" Gravy roared and smacked me on the ass again.

"Shit, bend me over baby, pleaseeee!" I begged as I felt my orgasm creeping up on me.

"Nah, juice this dick up!" he groaned.

"GRAVYYYYYYYYYYSHIIIIT!" I screamed and banged my hands against the walls. I didn't give a fuck who heard me because now that I was cuming, I was on savage mode.

Gravy swirled me over and bent me over my chair. I matched his stroke and began to squeeze the head of his dick while he fucked me. I felt him squeeze my hips tighter each time and his pace sped up.

"Ooohhhhh just like that, baby!" I moaned, looking at Gravy. He looked at me, and his sex face was so fucking sexy to me. Biting my lip, I knew he would lose it, and just as I thought, his bottom lip hung out his mouth as I felt him shoot all his babies inside me.

"Nah we ain't done yet, Jude."

Gravy sat in the chair I was just bent over, and he sat me on his dick facing him. He grabbed my breasts and feasted on them as I grabbed the back of the chair and began to ride his dick slowly. The feeling of Gravy biting my nipples had me ready to cum again, but I was trying to wait for Gravy this time. The competitive part of me wanted to make him cum first.

"Just like that, Jude." My breasts muffled his groans. I sped up a little using my pussy muscles to squeeze the base of his dick. "Chill ma before I nut," he said. I smiled and bent down to kiss him, speeding up some more. I knew it wouldn't be long now before he was cumming again.

"Cum in me, daddy!" I purred into his ear driving Gravy crazy. He squeezed my ass tighter and bit down hard on my neck as he filled me up some more. Gravy pulled my face down and kissed me passionately.

"I meant what I said, Fiona. I love you more than life itself, and with all your flaws I brought a few of my own. No matter what that test says or how my boys look, I love them just as much as I love you. Like Joshua, I'm going to war for them boys and the little girl I planted inside of you. I want my family back, and I will do whatever I have to keep them with me. Will you please be my wife, Fiona Jude?" Gravy reached below us and grabbed the ring out of his pocket. I knew Gravy meant what he said, and this time I made the right choice.

"Yes!" I said louder than I expected, covering my face as tears flooded them. Gravy sat forward again kissing me. I wanted this feeling to last forever because I was the happiest girl on the block right now. Gravy lifted me off him, and we both went and cleaned up as my phone rang. Since I missed the call, I went and grabbed my phone after getting dressed. Gravy lit a blunt while I checked the call. Seeing that it was my mother, I called right back.

The past year alone had drawn us closer. The first year was shaky because I was still rebellious. The things my mother would ask of me was out of the way, and she knew I wasn't down for that. I had quit the cleanup business, and my aunt was overjoyed because she didn't really like it, but she was also my biggest supporter. Pressing the send button I dialed my mother and wasn't ready for her to answer.

"What was the holdup Fiona, some dick?" she answered, and I burst out laughing.

"Ma, why would you say that? Where is daddy with you talking like that?" I asked, taking the blunt that Gravy passed me.

"He's in the living room. I'm cooking and was wondering if you were still coming. You didn't come the last two nights that we have invited you, and don't worry. I remember the boys were sick," Cari rambled, and I shook my head and listened. "I just wanna see my babies and your father some went out and bought Joshua that riding thing." She said, and I could see her rolling her eyes. Daddy had been bugged enough about a small four-wheeler that Joshua wanted, and I felt like he was too small, but Gravy and daddy agreed to show him how to ride it.

"Okay, well momma I'm going to get them ready now and head over." I smiled, passing the blunt back to Gravy.

"Thank you. Call your father. I love you." She ended the call, and I smiled. I texted my dad, and his response sent up concern.

"Baby something is wrong with my daddy." I showed Gravy the phone, and he looked confused. Frustrated, I snatched it back.

"What?" he yelled, throwing his hands in the air.

"Nothing, look. Ask Stephanie to watch the boys while we go by there. If it's nothing, I'll act like I was bringing a dish," I said, grabbing my pocketbook and keys.

"Man you tripping. Hurry up," Gravy growled, opening the door. I rolled my eyes as we walked out.

I went ahead to the car and Gravy went to talk to Stephanie. I was really concerned because my daddy never called me by my name. I mean ever. He would call me 'baby girl' or something similar. Daddy calling me Fiona had my antenna up, and I now felt an uneasy feeling about going there. Either way, I was on the way, so they better have been prepared and ready for whatever.

Gravy came out seconds later and started the car up.

"Now when we get here and ain't shit popping then I'm telling them the fucking truth with your crazy ass," Gravy joked, but I didn't see shit funny. I hoped that this was just a feeling, but I haven't felt this feeling in so long. But, I could never mistake it.

We got to my parents' home, and everything looked normal. Knocking on the door, I was surprised that no one came to the door. I looked back at Gravy, and he wasn't by the car or in the yard. My defenses went up because Gravy was right behind me.

"Babe! This shit ain't funny!" I yelled, walking around their yard.

I saw the side gate open and walked that way figuring he went to the back door. My mother had white roses planted through the walkway, but for some reason, they seemed so much more beautiful right now. I kept my pace still looking for Gravy when I started to hear soft music playing. I got to the backyard and saw all of our loved ones sitting and looking at me smiling. Gravy stood in a white and black tux, and my mother stood beside him smiling ear to ear with tears streaming down her face.

"I knew that response would get you here. Your mother owes me fifty bucks."

My daddy walked up in me looking amazing as well in his all-white tux. I saw all three boys run up to me and that's when I noticed the beautiful gown that laid along my body. My light skin flowed in this dress, and I could feel my tears trying to escape.

"Daddy, what is this?" I asked, looking over at him.

"The best day of your life, and you are well prepared for it. Come on, baby girl."

My father kissed my cheek and took my arm in his. We walked behind the boys who were all surprisingly calm. They stood beside Gravy, and I could see him smiling ear to ear. Gravy was sexy as fuck, and I couldn't believe they did all of this in so little time. I got to Gravy, and my father whispered something in his ear. Gravy chuckled and nodded while my father placed my hand in his.

"I'm going to kill you!" I joked, wiping the tears from my eyes.

"This was the only way. You peep everything else, ma." Gravy kissed my forehead. "I had to show you I was for real because talking wasn't working." He smiled, and I smiled back. I was literally at a loss for words. I couldn't believe I was about to marry Gravy. I never knew our connection would be this deep, but I can now admit that this is the happiest that I have been in a long time.

"Gerald tell her how you feel," Cari said, standing between us.

"To tell you how I fell you take an eternity. Fiona, you really are the air that I breathe. When you gave birth to MY boys that made me a better man. The past will stay right there because when I look into your green eyes, I only see our future. Your heart is so big, but look around." Gravy softly turned my head, and my tears continued to flow. "Your heart is that big to carry these people. You are the glue to all of us Fiona, and I am happy to make you my wife today in front of everyone who truly loves and cares for us. I love you, Fiona Jude Thomas," Gravy said, and I couldn't wipe my tears fast enough.

I couldn't talk, and my mother knew it because I was crying so much. I swear I didn't mean to be this dramatic, but this was all so sudden, and I was really in shock. Gravy's words hit me deep and to know that I had so much support meant the world to me. After getting myself together, the ceremony continued, and I married Gerald Thomas. We partied all night and when it was time for us to leave for our honeymoon, my mother pulled me aside.

"Fiona I just wanted to say thank you for letting me be a part of you, and the boys' lives after everything I have done. I know I've said this enough, but you mean the world to me and always will. I love you, Jude." Cari pulled me in for a hug, and I smiled.

"I love you too mommy. We are on the way to a bright future," I said, hugging her tighter. We pulled apart and joined everyone at the car for Gravy and me to leave. We waved goodbye and got into the car.

"We about to go in half on this little girl or nah?" Gravy asked, kissing my neck and playing with my clit.

"Name her Mercedes, baby," I moaned and laid my head back. Gravy twisted me and dove in head first. I watched him eat my pussy thinking this was the best curse a bitch could ask for.

The End